"Do you have a point, Mr...." She paused deliberately, still not looking him in the eyes.

"Rush. Ethan Rush," he said as smoothly and unself-consciously as if he were James Bond himself. "Do you recognise my name?"

"Should I?"

"Yes, I think you should."

She blinked and pushed the pack again to buy another moment of thinking time. Except she couldn't really think—she could barely breathe—and her pulse was pounding. "Well, I'm sorry, Mr. Rush, you'll have to explain."

"But you've been warned about me."

"I have?" Startled, she looked up—and found herself snared in the reddish tint of his brown eyes—the hardness of those eyes.

"Yes, on WomanBWarned. Do you know that website, Nadia?"

Oh yes, woman be warned. She knew his type: too good looking for his own good. The spoiled playboy who'd been outed as a two/three/four—or more—timer for sure. And he wasn't happy about it? Too bad.

Possibly the only librarian who got told off her-self for talking too much, **NATALIE ANDERSON** decided writing books might be more fun than shelving them—and, boy, is it that! Especially writing romance—it's the realization of a lifetime dream kick-started by many an afternoon spent devouring Grandma's Harlequin romance novels....

She lives in New Zealand, with her husband and four gorgeous-but-exhausting children. Swing by her website anytime—she'd love to hear from you: www.natalie-anderson.com.

**Other titles by Natalie Anderson available in ebook:**

**Harlequin Presents® Extra**

# DATING AND OTHER DANGERS

## NATALIE ANDERSON

~ Flirt Club ~

HARLEQUIN®

entertain, enrich, inspire™

Recycling programs
for this product may
not exist in your area.

ISBN-13: 978-0-373-52888-2

DATING AND OTHER DANGERS

First North American publication 2012

www.Harlequin.com

**Printed in U.S.A.**

# DATING AND
# OTHER DANGERS

To all the fabulous staff at Coffee Culture, Timaru—
who never mind when I sit in my favourite booth
for hours (and hours and hours), and who know
not to give me wifi access until I've done a decent
amount of work....

You guys are always so patient and friendly—
thanks heaps for giving my "office"
such great service!

# CHAPTER ONE

**WOMANBWARNED**
*Don't be a Doormat!*

*Sick of bad dates and being taken advantage of? Check the facts on him here first—and don't forget to tune into our latest tips to survive the dating jungle...*

***WomanBWarned*** *thread #1862: Mr 3 Dates and You're Out!*

**CaffeineQueen**—posted 15:49
*Ethan Rush might narrowly avoid screwing someone else at the same time, but he'll screw you over in a way that's worse. He's hot but he knows it—and totally fakes the charm. He'll take you somewhere flash a couple of times, flatter you 'til you can't think, give you the best sex ever. You're so dazzled. But before you know it he's saying goodbye. No explanation—just an "it was fun" note. He has to be setting up the next date while he's kissing off the last because next day he's out with her. He goes from the next to the next to the next. Don't fall for the irresistible act or try to catch because he'll never commit—3 dates and you're out.*

**MinnieM**—posted 18:23
*OMG, I dated him 2 and u r so right—he'll make u feel incredible but he'll never want more than 2 or 3 dates. Then u don't feel incredible. U feel like ur heart's been conned out of u. He's a total usr.*

**Bella_262**—posted 21:38
*He took me to this incredible restaurant. It was the most amazing night of my life. But for him? Who knows? All of a sudden it's over. I think he's just after numbers. I was so into him. Now I just feel like an idiot.*

**CaffeineQueen**—posted 07:31
*He had what he wanted and he went on his way. The fact that it was so good made it worse. You're left hanging, thinking you're half in love with him. And that there's something really wrong with you.*

**MinnieM**—posted 09:46
*I still don't know why he stopped calling. I thought it was going gr8 but no warning and is all over. Got amazing flowers but that really didn't help.*

**CaffeineQueen**—posted 10:22
*You got a bunch of flowers too? So did I. Definitely his standard MO. Bet there are heaps of others he's done it to. He's the one with the problem, ladies, not us. Avoid at all costs—don't let him get away with the playboy-rat routine any more!*

BENEATH his jeans and tee Ethan's skin burned hot one second and snap-froze the next as he read the website. He'd thought the link embedded in the e-mail his sister had sent would lead to the latest hilarious viral vid.

This wasn't hilarious. This was a horror-fest—all about him.

Mr 3 Dates and You're Out picked up the phone.

'Polly, you made this up,' he rapped, as soon as his sister answered.

'Sadly, no.' Polly sounded half-apologetic, half-teasing. 'You're *internetorious.*'

'But I don't use women.' The defensive instinct was impossible to suppress. 'No more than they use me,' he added when she didn't answer. 'I'm a generous date.' Good restaurant. Good company. Good time—for both parties.

'Generous in what way?' Polly asked. 'They're right. You never go on more than three dates with one woman. And you constantly date. *Constantly.*'

'And that's a problem because…?'

'You're only after one thing.'

'No, I'm not.' He enjoyed the company of women, but he didn't sleep around. 'I don't even go to bed with all of them.'

Polly's disbelieving silence echoed. Great. His own sister didn't believe him. Irritated, he glared at the computer, angered all the more by the petty words some bitter ex-dates had written about him. 'You cannot agree with this. Anyone can say anything they want on the internet. Where's the verification?'

'Well, I know the flowers thing is true.'

Because she was the florist he just about single-handedly kept in business. 'So that makes the rest of it true?'

His sister remained silent. Stupidly, it hurt more than it should—the way a paper cut made your eyes water despite being the smallest of incisions. He grimaced at the stupid cute logo with its blinding bright colours. 'Who does this, anyway? What kind of person sets up a website devoted to letting bitter and twisted women vent their vitriol?'

Hell had no fury, and the scorned woman behind this website must be one manipulative wench. She even had awful tee shirts for sale, so she could make money off the vulnerable and vindictive.

'Forget it, Ethan.' Polly tried to switch topic. 'I shouldn't have sent it to you. You're coming to the christening, right? Alone?'

'Yeah,' Ethan growled. 'So I can shield Mum from Dad's latest. And you were right to send it this to me, but off to believe it.' Eyes glued to the screen, he clicked on another couple of entries and seethed even more. He was on there with all the cheats and creeps—though that assumed that what these women claimed was actually true. He knew for sure *his* thread was fabrication, so he was sceptical. And increasingly furious.

'This is defamation.' The injustice burned. 'The internet might be all about free speech, but this is wrong.'

It was completely wrong. Damaging and dangerous. A site like this shouldn't be allowed. Someone had to do something about it before some guy's life or job was derailed by a bad online reputation.

Ethan Rush never shied from a challenge. And he didn't take *anything* lying down.

Nadia's eyes hurt as she squinted at her inbox. Staying up all night to moderate and update the forum had been such a dumb idea. And she'd had to come up with two new blog topics—which at three in the morning had been next to impossible. Her site had gotten so much bigger than she'd ever dreamed it would—truly fabulous—but it made focusing on the day job difficult. Unfortunately it was the day job that paid the bills. And it was the day job that was going to buy her the life and respect she'd fought for for ever. So she wasn't going to screw it up.

She closed her eyes and took a deep breath. Despite exercising on her way to work, there'd been no endorphin high, and she was going to need something more to get through the next eight hours. But before she could raid the snack machine for an assortment of fatty, sugary, salty, fifty-times-processed, plastic-wrapped rubbish, her phone rang.

'Nadia, I have a gentleman in reception asking for you,' Steffi the receptionist informed her, with an incredibly sparkly intonation.

'Really?' Nadia checked her calendar, but her first appointment wasn't scheduled for an hour. 'Me?'

'You. Apparently no one else will do.'

*Really?* Nadia didn't think so. He was probably a relentless wannabe recruit and Stef was fobbing him off on her. Millions wanted to work at Hammond Insurance. She knew. She'd fought like a wildcat to get her foot in the door.

'He's pretty insistent. Shall I send him through?'

Oh, yeah—Steffi was totally fobbing off some weirdo on her. 'Okay.' Nadia caved. 'Meeting room five, in three minutes.'

'Fantastic,' Steffi gushed.

Nadia frowned and lowered her voice to whisper into the phone. 'Stef, is everything okay?'

'Sure. Why?'

'You sound a little…puffed.'

'Oh, no.' Steffi laughed too loudly, all her breath seeming to blast down the phone. 'I'm *fine*!'

Uh-huh. Nadia hung up and swivelled her chair. She needed some screen-free time anyway. She picked up one of the recruitment packs and walked to the meeting room.

If he was a wannabe recruit Steffi could have given him

an info pack, but some of them were determined to talk to someone beyond Reception. Ah, well, it was a relief to delay starting properly, and she could raid the vending machine on her way back. She got to the meeting room and took up her position behind the desk. She flicked open the pack and prepared herself to deliver the bright smile and the spiel outlining the benefits of this amazing, ancient company, but not allowing too much hope to build in the guy. Hammond only took the best of the best. It took a hell of a lot of hard work to cut it here, and ninety-nine percent of people who applied never got over the threshold.

She looked up as a figure appeared in the doorway. She blinked at the brightness of Steffi's smile. The receptionist was flushed and sparkling, as if she'd had three too many glasses of champagne. She loudly told the person following her, 'Here's meeting room five!' then stepped to the side and Nadia saw the guy himself.

Cue several blinks in quick succession.

*So* not what she'd expected. She'd been thinking recent graduate—nervous, but bright. Sometimes they were youthfully brash, but they were never this smoothly confident, never this coolly controlled, never this kind of three thousand percent full-grown, red-blooded *man*. Sharp tailored suit, even sharper eyes, and a smile on the face that went with the prime male body. Nadia had never seen anyone with such perfect features in real life—that kind of symmetry was the domain of airbrushed aftershave ads. Only this guy had an edge that was *never* in those ads. No wonder Steffi had morphed into a breathless bimbo. Nadia's lungs squeezed helplessly in sympathy and she couldn't even manage an answering smile, let alone a hello. But the minute Steffi disappeared so did his smile.

A ripple skittered down Nadia's spine and her brain sharpened. She blinked away the blinding effect of his beauty. He didn't look as if he hoped to score a job at the most prestigious insurance firm in the city. He looked as if he had the world and its riches at his feet already, and could take or leave anything at his leisure. But that edge was there—*simmering*—and something raw was a scant centimetre below his incredibly smooth surface. Something she wasn't sure she wanted to identify.

He paused another moment just inside the doorway, then carefully closed the door behind him. All the while he stared as hard at her as she belatedly realised she was staring at him. Finally he spoke. '*You're* Nadia Keenan?'

She swallowed. 'That surprises you?' she asked, with a coolness that surprised her. She gestured to the seat across the table, because she was going to get a crick in her neck if she had to look that far up for another moment. Yeah, she should have stood, but her legs were as supportive as soggy tissue paper, and somehow she knew revealing weakness in front of this guy wouldn't be a smart idea.

He took the seat, moving his all-muscle, no-fat frame in a too controlled kind of way that made the ripples run even faster across her skin. Apprehension...and something else she *definitely* didn't want to identify. Instead her brain tracked down another avenue. Exactly how had he known to ask for her specifically? Because she was sure now he had—it wasn't Steffi fobbing anyone off. This guy was here for some very precise reason. But she was merely an HR assistant. It wasn't as if her name was listed on the company website. So why her?

Silence sharpened another second. She glanced past him, relieving her strained wide eyes and trying to regulate her pulse back to normal. Two of the walls were windows—the lower half frosted, but the upper part clear. Her clenched muscles eased a smidge. Anyone walking past could see in. There was no reason to feel isolated—

no reason to feel as if the room had been sucked of all its oxygen. There was no reason for those ripples to relentlessly slither back and forth across her skin. And it wasn't exactly fear…it was that something else.

She swallowed again and drew another cooling breath. 'How can I help—?'

'What's the policy on internet use here at Hammond?' he interrupted.

Pressing her lips together, she nudged the recruitment pack on the table between them, avoiding looking at him as she pulled her scattered thoughts together.

'I should imagine it's pretty conservative,' he continued, before she'd collated her answer. 'Pretty conservative establishment all round, is Hammond.'

'Do you have a point, Mr…?' She paused deliberately, still not looking him in the eyes.

'Rush. Ethan Rush,' he said, as smoothly and unselfconsciously as if he were James Bond himself. 'Do you recognise my name?'

'Should I?'

'Yes, I think you should.'

She blinked and pushed the pack again, to buy another moment of thinking time. Except she couldn't really think—she could barely breathe—and her pulse was *pounding*. 'Well, I'm sorry, Mr Rush, you'll have to explain.'

'But you've been warned about me.'

'I have?' Startled, she looked up—and found herself snared in the reddish tint of his brown eyes—the *hardness* of those eyes.

'Yes, on WomanBWarned. Do you know that website, Nadia?'

In less than the micro-second it took for her to gasp, shock had covered her body in goosebumps. Every inch of her skin screamed with sensitivity; every cell was shot with adrenalin. She let another second slide, and as it did she decided to avoid—then feign ignorance. And if that failed she'd deny, deny, deny.

'Was there something you needed today, Mr Rush?'

'Yes, I wanted to be sure about the internet policy here at Hammond, and apparently you're the HR expert on it.' He didn't seem to move, but he was somehow even bigger, filling the room with ferocious energy. 'Tell me,' he said drily, 'does your employer know you run one of the bitchiest, most defamatory sites on the internet?'

Nadia's throat tightened as if a hangman's noose had just been jerked, rendering speech impossible.

'It wouldn't do your little HR role much good if your bosses found out about your hobby, would it? Not when you're sending out these little edicts to all their employees about online protocol. Not in a great position to give advice, are you?'

Nadia firmed her jaw—she resented the "hobby" description.

He pulled a paper from his pocket and unfolded it, placing it in the table. She glanced at the heading, and then back up to his simmering countenance. She didn't need to read more because she'd written most of it. The internal memo on internet access and computer use, explicitly detailing that social networking sites, forums and such, were forbidden. She'd drafted the updated policy before getting it approved by Legal and her supervisors.

'Where did you get that?' And how on earth had he tracked her down?

'I find it so ironic that you deliver seminars to the other employees about protecting their online presence and reputation when you're so vicious in cyberspace yourself.'

'Do you have a point, Mr Rush?' She curled her toes

and tensed her muscles. She wanted to escape but refused to run away. Because she really needed to know what his point was. Despite her hammering heart, she told herself to keep calm. She was safe. She'd never used Hammond computers for her forums and she never would—her job mattered too much.

'What do you think, Nadia? Why am I here?'

She shrugged her shoulders slightly. 'No reason I can think of. Unless you wish to discuss possible employment at Hammond, I don't think we have anything to say to each other.'

He smiled as he surveyed her. Sitting back in his seat, he was now completely at ease, as if he was the one who worked here, and not total stranger who'd just come in off the street. And he was completely gorgeous, in an all-male, all-arrogant way.

Oh, yes—woman be *warned*. She knew his type—too good-looking for his own good. A spoilt playboy who'd been outed as a two/three/four or more timer for sure. And he wasn't happy about it? Too bad.

His eyes compelled her to answer his challenge. Fire burned in them—literally a touch of russet in the cinnamon iris—impossible to ignore.

But she'd damn well try. 'You might be twice my size, but you don't intimidate me. You can take your threatening attitude elsewhere.'

'Threatening?' He laughed. The sound spiked the air with danger. 'I'm not here to threaten, Nadia. I'm here to extract a promise.'

She quickly touched her tongue to the inside of her dry lips.

'The thread about me is defamatory,' he said bluntly.

'Well…' She forced a smile. 'The defence to defamation is truth.'

'That's right,' he agreed.

'So you're saying what's on there *isn't* the truth?'

'That's right.'

She shrugged. 'So prove it.'

Six seconds passed by. Her senses had suddenly grown so acute she could hear the hand of her tiny watch ticking, so she knew exactly.

'You don't think that's the wrong way round Nadia? In a free and just legal system a man is innocent until proven guilty. But in the little world *you've* created he's guilty until proven innocent. You don't see a problem with that?'

She shot him a look designed to wither. 'The men detailed on my site *are* guilty.'

*His* answering glare was withering and then some. 'You don't accept that it might be open to abuse? You don't think a woman with a vendetta might take advantage of it?'

'A woman with a vendetta? Please—men like you made up that kind of stereotype.'

'So you're *not* a woman who was hurt by some man and seeking payback? That isn't why you set this thing up?'

Her temper flared. 'I set this up so people had access to information. All kinds of information.'

'Because all men are bastards?'

'Information about dating in the modern world,' she corrected. But this conversation was futile. He was never going to understand—clearly his outsize ego was too bruised. 'I don't need to justify myself to you.'

'Oh, I think you do.' He leaned forward. 'I think you need to justify your actions to a lot of people. And why won't you come clean about it? Why hide behind online anonymity? Your employers here don't even know.'

She glanced out of those windows, wishing they were solid walls now. Of course they didn't know. They'd totally disapprove. They stressed online responsibility and reputation—it was what *she* taught every new recruit. And she did not want to jeopardise her job. She'd worked too hard to get it.

'I don't cheat,' he said firmly. 'And I don't swindle naïve girls out of their life savings. So why am I on there?'

'You've obviously hurt someone.' And she'd be reading the thread to find out how, the second she got the chance.

'So where's my right of reply?'

'You can post a rebuttal. You just have to register and log in.'

'What? And give myself an anonymous identity like the shrews on there?' He shook his head. 'I think *you* need to take ownership of the site that you've created. *You* need to take responsibility for the accuracy of the content and for the damage that can ensue from it.'

'In what way has it damaged you?' He struck her as bulletproof.

He paused. 'Reputation is an unquantifiably precious thing.'

She knew that. 'So what do you want?'

He sat back in his seat, the back of his fingers brushing his mouth and jaw. She tried very hard not to follow the movement and focus on that mouth with its full lips. Instead she tried to meet his gaze—except it seemed it had wandered…

She watched, steaming up, as he looked at her mouth, her neck, her chest. She saw the deepening fire in his expression and felt the response inside herself—her muscles shifting as hormones rushed. Beneath her blouse her breasts tightened…

Of course her body would react to just a look from this too handsome playboy stud. Her mating instinct was so *off*.

Slowly his lashes lifted and he captured her gaze with

his gleaming one. 'I guess if I have to prove it, then I'll prove it.'

'How are you going to do that?' And why was she suddenly whispering?

'Three dates,' he said, just as softly.

'Pardon?'

'You and I are going to go out on three dates. You're the judge, jury and the executioner, right? So judge me on the facts. I'll prove to you that what's up on your site is untrue.'

She laughed—only one note lower than hysterical. It was preposterous. 'I'm not dating you.'

'It's that or call your lawyers.' His gaze coasted over her again, assessing in the most base way. 'Got lots of money for lawyers, Nadia? No, of course you don't. Otherwise why would you be working as a lowly HR assistant?'

'The users of my forum sign a waiver.' She tried to recover her ground. 'I can't be held responsible for what they put up there.'

'It's so convenient for you to hide behind that rule, isn't it? I think it could be due for a test in court, though.' He smiled sympathetically. 'And it'll take months. All that time off work… Everyone here at work is going to know, Nadia. And your family, friends…' His eyes narrowed. 'They don't know either, do they?' He went for the kill. 'You're going to need good lawyers for a long and expensive time, honey.'

'You're willing to waste that money yourself?' Her stomach churned. He couldn't be serious. Surely he wouldn't do that?

'I don't think it is a waste. Anyway, I *am* a lawyer, I can represent myself.'

Of course he was a lawyer. He was every inch an aggressive, adversarial jerk. Well, he wasn't going to intimidate *her*. She swallowed back the bile burning its way up her throat. 'I'm not taking your thread down. It's freedom of speech.'

'Actually, I don't want you to take it down,' he said thoughtfully. 'Let's face it, once things are out there on the web they're out there for ever. What I want is a retraction.'

'Then you need to contact the woman you slimed, not me.' He didn't need to involve *her* at all. Three dates? It was ridiculous.

'They're anonymous—I don't know who they are.'

*They?* Oh, how very nice. 'And you can't figure it out because there are so many possibilities?' She widened her eyes in fake surprise. 'Be honest.' She snapped into attack mode. 'What you really want is a suck-up piece, going on about how fabulous you are in bed.'

'You're offering to sleep with me so you can report with accuracy?'

Her face went hot. So did every other part of her body.

'I don't need your approval to know my worth as a lover, Nadia. What I want is an acknowledgement that sometimes people put things up there with a warped perspective. Although what I *really* want is for you to pull the plug on this poisonous swamp of bitterness altogether.'

'That's not going to happen.'

'Being a bitch is that important to you?'

She shrugged. 'If warning other women about jerks who want to use them makes me a bitch, then I'm happy to be considered one. For a long time.'

'So how do you know what they put up is accurate?'

'Why would anyone lie?' It was simple. 'I've already told you these aren't women with a vendetta. These are women who've been hurt really badly.'

'Women like you?'

She froze for a nano-second. 'It isn't personal for me.'

'Like hell it isn't.'

Grimly, she hid her fists beneath the desk and tried to think of a way out. But she was backed into a corner and she knew it. 'Okay, then. You want three dates? Fine. But we go Dutch.'

He winced theatrically, but that didn't hide the satisfaction in his eyes. 'Yeah, you would be that crass.'

'I wouldn't want to feel I owed you anything, Mr Rush. Or that you expected anything from me because you bought me an expensive dinner.'

'Actually, I'm expecting quite a lot from you Nadia.' He smiled with genuine amusement. 'And call me Ethan.'

She stood up and walked to the door, because if she didn't her anger was going to burst out utterly inappropriately. He stood too. She saw him take in her height and glance down to register the height of her heels. She just knew he was mentally calculating the difference if the shoes were off.

'Very dangerous things come in small packages,' she said tightly.

He grinned—the patronising, "amused by the little girl" grin that she'd seen way too many times in her life.

'So do very precious things,' he countered softly.

She didn't see him the rest of the way out. Couldn't. The wave of heat all but blinded her. Half fury, half something else altogether. Oh, yes, he deserved to be on WomanBWarned, even if he wasn't a bona fide candidate. He'd trample hearts without any effort whatsoever.

But not hers. Never, *ever* hers.

# CHAPTER TWO

**WomanBWarned**
*Top tips for surviving the dating jungle. What not to do on your first date...*

*Don't drink—at least not much. Alcohol impairs judgment and you want to make safe, sensible decisions.*

*Don't be too sexual—if it's a possible relationship you want, not a one night hook-up, then keep a little mystery. You want to be taken seriously.*

*Don't go on and on about your ex(es) or your ailments or how awful your boss is. Negativity is a downer.*

*Don't go to the movies—it's a cop-out. You want to get to know the person, not sit next to them in silence for two hours.*

*Don't try too hard—just relax and be yourself.*

ETHAN sprawled on the sofa in his apartment and laughed as he read, his laptop balanced his stomach. Oh, boy! *OlderNWiser*—the online pseudonym for one Nadia

Keenan—really had her rules, didn't she? There were a ton of little blog bits on her site, giving tips for this and that in the dating realm. As if she was some kind of expert.

He *so* didn't think so.

The woman needed a lesson or fifty from a true master. And he knew just how he was going to do it—by taking over her own turf, of course. Fighting fire with fire and all that. Because anyone could set up a blog, right? And fortunately he was partner at a firm that *didn't* have uptight HR princesses like Nadia Keenan. His firm believed in treating adults like adults, and didn't care about what personal things employees decided to put up on the internet. There were no draconian, moralistic guidelines attempting to govern their workers' private lives. So long as it wasn't work-related, and didn't impact negatively on the business, they weren't interested. If the people he did deals with stumbled across it they'd most likely laugh and cheer him on. They were human, with senses of humour.

Yeah, it wasn't because of *his* work that he was bothered by her reputation-shredding website. For him, it was the core injustice of having to prove innocence instead of guilt. That violation of a fundamental legal principle. Okay, there was an element of the personal too. They'd picked on the wrong Rush. Ethan didn't deserve to be slated—it was his father who was the jerk. And Ethan refused to be anything like his father—not fickle, not deceitful, not hurtful. Ethan might play, but he was up-front and honest about it, and always nice to the women whose company he enjoyed. Mind you, he didn't feel like being nice to Nadia Keenan.

He logged onto one of the major blogging sites and thought for a second about a title.

GuysGetWise?

Fantastic—not registered, and his to use.

And his tagline?

*Taking on the Dirt-Dishing Dating Divette.*

He could do alliteration too, see? And at least he could spell, rather than use basically illiterate abbreviations. The t-crossing, i-dotting legal writer in him detested those. Although admittedly "divette" was his own invention—but she was too itty-bitty to be a true diva. He filled in the little grid detailing "all about this blog"…

*Ethan Rush—supposedly "shamed" as Mr 3 Dates and You're Out over on WomanBWarned wants those women to get real and for guys to wise up to the dating reputation dross that's online. Come hang out here, boys, and get clued up to the reality. And get way better dating advice than any you'll read over there…*

Because he was so much more of an expert on dating than Ms OlderNWiser, and she was going to know it. He chuckled as he composed his first entry. There was nothing like a direct challenge to get his blood pumping. Grin wolfish, he started typing the beginning…

**GuysGetWise**: *The chick flick is your friend*

*According to the self-proclaimed guru over at **WomanBWarned**, **OlderNWiser**, going to the movies is a dumb first date destination.*
*Wrong.*
*    A cinema is a nice, totally safe environment that can push the defrost button on even the most hardened ice queen—like **OlderNWiser** herself.*
*You can round it out more if you want by going for pizza before, if necessary—NOT the usual cheap delivery, guys. This first time it's got to be gourmet. Be seen to be making an effort. But, as we all*

*know, there's nothing worse than being stuck at a pricey restaurant with a vacuous woman who has no conversation while waiting hours for two strips of potato, a fifty-pence-sized piece of steak and some weird green oil drizzled in dots on the edge of an oversized white plate. Instead go for pizza to say hi, and then ease off the pressure for a bit.*

*The movie gives you a couple of hours to settle into each other's company—you're close, but not too intensely focused on each other. Afterwards you've got something to talk about to start you off. And then, once she's started, she won't stop. Babes like to talk—and they will if warmed up. After a movie she'll be in the mindset. So let her share with you.*

*Immutable dating fact: the more you let her share, the more she'll want to be with you. It's that simple.*

*You might wince, but the chick flick in particular is your friend. She'll get the warm fuzzy feeling. Go for the one-two punch—the chick flick followed by dessert. She'll be as gooey inside as the chocolate pudding she's spooning in. And, bud, you will benefit from the happy ending hormones she's riding on.*

*Brace yourselves and get her to a rom-com, feel-good kissy flick. That's what I'll be doing with Ms* **OlderNWiser**. *It's the perfect first date softener. And us guys like soft.*

Ethan paused, his fingers hovering above the keyboard, his lips twisting as an evil urge gripped him.

*Stay tuned for how to nail her on the second date.*

He hit "publish" before he had second thoughts. Hey, he'd said it all along—there was a lot of rubbish out there on the internet. And she'd shredded his rep anyway, right? This was his way of reclaiming his own image. He didn't really give a damn about what the anonymous readers on the ends of the ethernet thought, but he was *not* a cheat—yes, he played, but all the playmates had fun. And he'd get even the world's most uptight woman to appreciate some *fun*…

His blood quickened, but he forced his brain to stay open for duty. He went into the WomanBWarned site and registered—under his own name—and then went to the *Mr 3 Dates and You're Out* thread to comment.

> *EthanRush: Looking for another side to this little story? What happened to balance and verification of information? Neither of those things are apparent on this bitch-fest. So how about a challenge? The woman in WomanBWarned herself— OlderNWiser—has agreed to a series of dates with me, Mr 3 Dates and You're Out. As she's Chief Judge and Executioner around here, she's agreed to give me a fair trial.*
> 
> *Three dates, of course.*
> *She'll play them her way. I'll play them mine.*
> *We'll report back and you can decide—who's the honest one and who's the user?*
> *Who's the victor?*

The comment appeared beneath all the others. He'd well and truly thrown down the gauntlet. What he needed now were some supportive comments to get traffic his way and stack the odds in his favour. Happily, he had some guys who knew him well enough to know his tongue was—partly—in his cheek. Guys liked sport, and he was a team player. His team would get behind him. He put the link on his social networking page, then shut the laptop and closed his eyes.

And then it hit him.

This was *mad*. This wasn't what was supposed to have happened. He was supposed to have gone in there all guns blazing and torn shreds off her. Demand she take down the thread, take down the whole damn site, and totally threaten to sue her.

Okay, he *had* threatened that.

But only after he'd been struck by a far more entertaining idea. The threat had simply been a way to push her into accepting that far more entertaining idea. With her *OlderNWiser* handle he'd figured he'd be facing down some ancient hardened up crone, but in reality she looked like one of the fairies on his three-year-old niece's miniature china teaset. All fine bones and fine features in her heart-shaped face, with her hair tumbling loose and kinking at the ends. And, yes, his thoughts *had* immediately kinked.

He'd have to be careful how he played this, because he refused to end up in a mess. He did charming and nice—never messy. But he'd teach her a lesson—Nadia Keenan was going *down*.

No, *not* sex—there'd be no sliding along sun-kissed limbs, no stroking delicate collarbones, no relentlessly touching 'til she begged for mercy and then screamed her ecstasy in his mouth. No matter how vivid that fantasy was, an even bigger temptation bit. He'd get her hot and twisted and then be a total gentleman. Restraint all the way. And she'd hate him even more than she already did.

He couldn't get over the contradiction—she looked sweet but she savaged people with her vindictive website. Who'd hurt her, and how? She'd said it wasn't personal, but there *had* to have been a guy who'd broken what little heart she had. Her online ID even acknowledged she was *OlderNWiser*.

He flipped the laptop open again, went back to *WomanBWarned* and clicked on the archives link.

To win any game you had to be prepared. You had to understand your opponent's weakness…

Nadia wished Megan was home, but she was in Greece for three weeks, meeting her boyfriend Sam's family, meaning the flat they shared was quiet and empty and totally lacking in advice—the walls weren't answering back.

She pushed aside the clothes-hangers in her wardrobe, desperately searching despite knowing exactly what items were there and that whatever it was she wanted wasn't.

Because she didn't know *what* she wanted and she didn't have the funds to shop.

She had to ace it over Ethan Rush, but he had every angle covered. Good looking, intelligent, loaded—that was obvious from his clothes and his confidence. Everything came easily to him—even her acquiescence to his stupid idea. She had to shake him from his self-satisfied, smug little perch. But how?

She picked up the bag she'd tossed on her bed. Her phone rang just as she got hold of it. Megan—hooray for serendipity.

'What do I wear to a date I don't want to go on?' Nadia asked straight off.

'A date?' Megan's high-pitched amazement was no surprise. 'Why don't you want to go?'

'Because he's a complete jerk who's bullied me into it.'

'Nadia,' Megan scoffed, 'no one bullies you.'

Ten hours ago Nadia would have agreed. 'If I don't date him he says he's going to sue me for defamation and out me as the woman behind WomanBWarned.'

'Don't tell me he's on it?'

'Yeah—has his own thread. *Mr 3 Dates and You're Out.* Totally smooth snake who's only interested in sex. Moves on immediately after. Serial dating offender, seriously arrogant. More than one victim has commented.'

'He used *that* to get you to agree to go on a date with him?'

'Three dates.'

'*Three?*' Megan started to giggle. 'Oh, he's good.'

'He's not good. He's mad.'

'But he won't waste money suing. Just tell Hammond you run the site. They won't care. It's in your own hours and on your own equipment.'

'I worked too hard to get that job. I'm not screwing it up.' Independence mattered—achievement mattered. Nadia wasn't failing now, having secured a great flat and a great job when no one in her family had believed a "little thing" like her could—or, worse, *should*. They'd thought a big city was too bad a place for her, so she'd gone to the biggest city in the country and got employed by one of the biggest, most traditional-to-a-T firms. That was the only way she could to prove herself to them—they'd just be baffled by her blog.

'I'm reading the thread. He sounds interesting.' Megan drew in a long, slow breath. 'Good sex. When did you last have sex?'

Nadia banged the wardrobe door shut. It was all right for Megan. She and Sam were still in that honeymoon phase, so she was getting it at least twice a day. Nadia hadn't had it twice in the last year. Or two.

'Nadia.' Megan's tone totally changed. 'Did you see his reply?'

Nadia's blood iced up. 'There wasn't one.' She ran into the lounge, where her computer dominated the dining table. Praise be to high-speed broadband, because the thread loaded in a flash. And it only took a flash to realise what he'd done.

'He's made it public. The dates.' Her throat clogged. 'Why? Everyone is going to know we're going out.' And there was going to be a *victor*? Oh, she'd been right. This was war.

'Well, they know *he* is.' Megan morphed into the voice of calm. 'You've still got your anonymous ID. There's a link to a blog. He has a blog?'

'It's new, and I'm already reading it,' Nadia said grimly, quickly skimming the post and growing all the more aggravated.

But Megan giggled. 'I can't wait for him to "nail" you on the second date.'

'He's a conceited jerk. He's not nailing anything.' Certainly not her. And she certainly wasn't feeling a quiver of excitement at the thought. The quiver was suppressed rage.

'He's good-looking, right?' Megan asked. 'He must be to be this confident.'

'If you like over-sized macho men who think they're it and everything else.' Physical invincibility didn't do their personalities any favours, and she didn't need the over-protectiveness that tended to accompany their delusions of demi-god status.

'He sounds just the ticket.' Megan had pepped up. 'What *are* you going to wear?'

Nadia bit back her growl. She knew Megan wanted her to be as loved-up and happy as she was, but she didn't want to be attractive to Ethan—she wanted armour. Fortunately high-pitched beeps interrupted whatever Megan was saying now.

'I have to go, Meg,' Nadia said quickly. 'I've got another call.' She jabbed the buttons. 'Hello?'

'Nadia.'

From the frying pan to the fire. Just her luck. 'Ethan.' Those infernal goosebumps smothered her skin. She refused to recognise the other instant reaction deep and low in her belly.

'Wednesday night good for you?' No preamble or polite chit chat—but his voice was caramel enough.

Wednesday. Mid-week and only two days away. She needed more prep time. 'Actually, I already have plans for Wednesday,' she lied. She wasn't going to make it easy for him. Not at all.

'Thursday, then?'

'I could do Thursday.'

'I was thinking a movie or something.'

Total fail on the originality front, but she'd get him back—because she'd read his stupid blog. She wasn't going to let him know she'd read it. Damn. She suddenly realised that he would know if he checked his traffic stats and knew her ISP. Which he obviously did—he seemed to know way too much about her internet activity. She quickly took a screenshot and logged out of the site. She'd only check it from wireless hotspots now, at random coffee bars or something.

'That sounds great,' she said with zero enthusiasm. 'Can I choose the movie?'

'Of course.'

She paused. 'How did you get my number?'

'Same way I found out you're the woman behind WomanBWarned. There's a lot of information out there on the internet.'

'But it's secure.'

'Never as secure as you think. I'll pick you up from your place.'

'You know where I live?' Now, *that* was scary.

'Sure.' She could hear his smile. 'On the corner of Bitter and Twisted Street, right?'

'What a shame you won't *get lost*.'

'I don't plan to,' he drawled, in a way that made her shiver more. 'Text me all your details and I'll let you know what time.'

'Oh, I can't wait,' she cooed, just to get the last word in.

She tossed her phone onto the sofa and stared at the words frozen on her huge screen. It was the "divette" that did it. The patronising, belittling, condescending bastard.

Damn it, she *was* going shopping. She wanted to look more than nice. She wanted to look *hot*. So hot he couldn't help but want her and make his one move too many. The possibility was there—she'd seen the flash in his expression when he'd looked her over so boldly in her office today. Definite sparks. And she didn't deny she'd responded on a basic level. But she could control her own reaction while blowing harder on those sparks. Get *him* hot. And then—when he made his move—she'd refuse him. And that would be so incredibly satisfying.

Nadia wasn't conceited, but she didn't underestimate her potential strengths either. She knew she had a little something that intrigued some men. *Little* being the operative word. A lot of guys liked petite women. Funnily enough, it was often the taller guys who liked petite women most. Nadia figured it made them feel all the more manly. Men like that loved to be looked up to. Literally.

Ethan the Arrogant would definitely like being looked up to.

So she'd do the pretty little woman thing and emphasise her femininity. She went back to the WomanBWarned thread and looked at the comments from the women who'd dated him. She was curious to know more—as moderator she could e-mail them and surreptitiously try to get more info. A possibility she'd definitely keep on file. But if what they said was true then a move from Ethan was probably inevitable, no matter what she wore. Sexual conquest was as natural to him as breathing. It wasn't that he was interested in the individual woman—it was the chase that thrilled him. Pure predator.

But she wanted to turn the screws on him as hard as she could, so she had to make herself more attractive prey. Because she was going to be the woman to put him in his place.

# CHAPTER THREE

SHE had found the best ever dress. Not evening formal, but floaty, floral and ultra-feminine. A little pricey, but it was worth it. She teamed it with soft ballerina flats rather than strappy heeled sandals, to really highlight the height thing. She normally never wore anything less than two inches outside her front door, but she was prepared to make a few sacrifices for this mission. She left her hair loose, wearing a slim scrunchie as a bracelet in case it got hot on her neck and she wanted to tie some of it back. She had a soft wrap for her shoulders and a dainty little bag hanging from her shoulder. Minimal make-up—mascara, a little eyeliner, and pink-tinted gloss on her lips.

Fresh, feminine, an innocent at large—that was the look she was going for.

As she'd expected, he turned up right on time. When she heard the knock on the door she had an overwhelming urge not to answer, but she flicked her hair back and faked a smile. It died the second she saw him, and anger flared in its stead. How dared the guy be so hot-looking? Staggeringly perfect, in a steely, square-jawed kind of way—not to mention tall and broad and big in terms of presence. Immaculately dressed in casual jeans and a cotton tee that showed off his shoulders and abs, he just didn't seem real. No wonder he thought he could sail through women without a care—it happened all too easily for him to realise otherwise. Her confidence evaporated in the face of his undeniable attractiveness. Who did she think she was kidding? Could she really play with fire this hot?

'I thought we could get some pizza before we go to the movies,' he said. Amusement and satisfaction lurked in his eyes.

She stiffened as she saw the smugness, and her game plan zipped back. The urge to better him overwhelmed her. She'd do it whichever way she could.

'Oh, that would have been great...' She let her voice trail and frowned a little.

'But?' he prompted.

'Well, the thing is, a movie I've been wanting to see for ages is on, and to catch it we need to go straight to the theatre.' She deliberately bit her bottom lip and looked up, up, up at him, with wide, wide eyes. 'Do you mind?' she asked, as softly and breathily as a 1960s screen starlet— she hoped, anyway.

He didn't answer for a long moment, that lurking light of amusement completely snuffed. 'That's...not a problem.' He half turned away. 'Shall we go now, then?'

'Oh, come in for a moment,' she said with a sweet smile, aiming to appear as accommodating as possible. 'I need to get my wrap.'

It was a warm summer night and she *so* didn't need the wrap—she was boiling. But after half an hour in the movies she always ended up freezing, and she had no intention of snuggling next to him for some heat, despite her plan to fire up the flirt between them.

'Thanks.' He sounded surprised. He looked surprised. She glanced back and saw him taking in the bright surroundings. She knew the flat was stylish and welcoming. But he made rooms shrink when he stood in them, and he made both the background and colours fade—so her focus was forced towards him.

'You've got a nice place.'

Nadia picked up the pashmina that she'd artfully draped on the edge of the large, soft sofa. 'You thought I'd live alone in some dreary bedsit?' Like the lonely, bitter spinster he believed she was? She'd known he'd think that, so she'd deliberately put a slide show of pictures from one of her and Megan's riotous trips to France on her computer. What was it with people pigeon-holing her? Her own parents had told her she shouldn't move to London—that the city was too big for her. The only thing that was too big was the price of the rent. But she had a job at a fabulous firm and sharing this place with Megan was worth it.

His smile grew as he watched a few pictures glide across the screen. 'I'm a fast learner, Nadia. And I'm learning to expect the unexpected with you.'

'Really?'

'Sure.' He faced her. 'So let's get going.'

Adrenalin zinged. She followed him out and locked the door. They walked down the path a few metres before he hailed a cab. She was surprised—for some reason she'd thought he'd have a car.

'You don't like to go by cab?' He caught her hesitation as he opened the door.

Truth was, she didn't want to sit in the back with him. It felt intimate—she'd have preferred to be in separate seats, with a drinks holder between them. Sharing this one space made all kinds of inappropriate images flash—namely, snogging in the back seat.

She banished the wild idea, crossed her knees and ankles, and crouched into the corner, firmly telling both her body and her thoughts to settle down. He relaxed across his half, not taking up more than his fair share. But it felt like it. He was angled towards her. She didn't look at him but could feel him willing her to. She sighed and gave in, registering his slight smile.

'You look lovely, by the way,' he said suavely. 'Very beautiful.'

'Thanks,' she said without meaning it. 'You look good too. But you already know that.'

'Well, *you* know you look incredible no matter what you wear.' His smile teased. 'But isn't it nice to be told anyway?'

She just rolled her eyes.

'Compliments don't work for you?' He looked all the more amused.

'Not from you,' she said bluntly—despite it being partly untrue. 'This whole date thing is a really stupid idea, don't you think? I'm not going to believe a word you say because all you want to do is impress me so I'll say you're a great guy and how wrong all those women are.'

'The circumstances don't matter,' he argued calmly. 'I bet you're a tough woman to impress at the best of times.'

'What makes you say that?' She shrank into an even tighter ball.

His gaze locked on her, and she stiffened at the dispassionate, intensely assessing expression.

'I think you live life according to a list of rules,' he said. 'Many lists of rules. Like the first date protocol you posted on your forum. You have rules for everything— like the uptight HR assistant you are. And anyone who doesn't meet those rules is an auto-fail. There's no room for human error in your life.'

'That's not true.' Her life was strewn with human error—mostly her own.

'No?' A faint smile. 'You're saying sometimes you don't follow your own advice?'

'The little advice I offer comes from my own experience. I'd be a fool to repeat my past mistakes.'

He nodded as if she'd confirmed something. 'So you've turned into a coward.'

Nadia's blood heated even more. 'I'm not a coward, but I am cautious. And I'm not going to apologise for that.'

'Yes, but it strikes me you're a very intelligent, capable woman. Maybe you should have more faith in yourself.'

'Oh, please.' He was back to the complimenting already? This was all part of his charm attack.

'Seriously, you should give your instincts free rein— let yourself go.'

'Oh, you would say that,' she said witheringly. 'That's your aim—for women to let down all their defences *in your arms*.' She shook her head. 'So you flatter and listen and smile your charming smile—and wait for the cherries to fall right into your mouth. It's all so damn *false*.'

His jaw dropped, then he shut it again. Had she actually hit home with that one?

'All right then.' He cleared his throat. 'I won't try to impress you.'

She should have felt a spurt of satisfaction, but the wretched thing was he didn't need to *try* to impress. His very existence did that—he was beyond blessed with physical attributes, and had a voice that demanded attention. Even worse, some of what he said was of interest. Okay, compelling. She'd bet he was a brilliant lawyer.

Why was her stupid radar tuned to men filled with maximum virility when the simple presence of such sensual drive meant they couldn't possibly keep it zipped? Giving in to her instincts would have her as easily obtainable as all the other women he'd encountered. So she'd have to fight against them all the harder.

'So tell me about the movie.' He switched to neutral ground.

'I've been meaning to see it for ages.' She hid her smile as she thought of what was in store.

They got to the small independent theatre and were directed to the smallest viewing room. There was only them and one other person at the screening. She'd done a whole five minutes of research to find the worst-sounding movie on in London, and within three minutes of the film rolling she knew she'd succeeded.

It was in French, with subtitles so crooked they were unreadable, and about the tortured lives of an artist, his wife and his lover. And it was torture to watch. Lots of scenes with the artist painting—they literally got to watch paint dry.

After only ten minutes Nadia was beside herself with boredom and hoping Ethan was going as insane as she was. But she wasn't fidgety just because the on-screen action was mind-numbing. She was hyper-aware of him. They were too close in this darkened space. And the worst of it was the film was just over three hours in duration—that was why she'd picked it. But now she had to sit so near to a man who attracted her body as much as he repelled her mind. And three hours was beyond torture.

The artist scratched his thin brush on canvas for another hour or so. Oh, it was so bad—but it would be worth it. Ethan would hate it as much as she did. They'd both come out of it grumpy, and that served him right for thinking he'd "soften" her up with a movie. A chick flick? Hell no.

But wait a second. He was *chuckling*. She'd missed the wonky subtitle on that bit. She glanced sideways to read his expression in the flickering light. It appeared that he was completely absorbed in the movie, while she was almost out of her tree. The frankly useless artist worked for hours, mostly in silence. Occasionally he muttered in French. Hang on, that was *Ethan* muttering something in French—what? She glanced at him. He was smiling again, as if the movie was the most entertaining thing ever. How was watching paint dry even remotely fun?

And then, to her horror, the so thrilling action was finally interrupted—by an incredibly raw sex scene, featuring the artist and his lover. Not graphic, but so passionate and uncontrolled she felt like a voyeur. She sat completely still, as every cell burned up, and seriously wanted to escape. She shut her eyes but the sounds haunted her—and images popped into her head. But no longer was it the scrawny artist—no, it was the fit, filled frame of six foot *several* inches Ethan.

Oh, no, no, no—she was not imagining him. And her. She was *not*.

She was so glad when the guy went back to his painting. Ten minutes of that settled her pulse again. But then there was another sex scene—a way more graphic one. The action was really ramping up now—this time with the wife. Only in the middle of all the puffing and panting Nadia's stomach started rumbling—loud enough to be heard despite the sudden ecstatic shrieks of the woman.

Even though she'd known she was going to refuse Ethan's pizza offer, she hadn't eaten before he arrived—the butterflies hip-hopping in her stomach had made that impossible. So now she coughed to cover the uncontrollable gurgling sound, but that was somehow worse as the couple on screen kept right on rutting each other. She buried her face in her hand and simply wanted to die. Why hadn't she checked the rating comments on the film and picked up on the high sexual content warning?

'Are you not feeling well?' Ethan asked solicitously—leaning uncomfortably close.

'I'm fine,' she ground out between gritted teeth, quickly glancing up, only to see total laughter glinting in his eyes.

Damn.

Finally the credits rolled—not fast enough—and apparently Ethan was a watch-them-till-the-end man. It wasn't until the lights went on, bright and unforgiving, that he turned and gave her an even higher wattage smile.

'Was it as good as you'd hoped?' he asked.

'Oh, yes,' she lied as she stood and marched out of there. 'So you speak French?' Of all the rotten luck.

'*Mais oui*, of course.' He held the exit door for her. 'Shame you don't, because some of the subtleties were lost in translation, I thought it was a very interesting film.'

'Really?'

'No, it was rubbish.' He let the door slam behind them. 'But that was the point, right?'

So he knew. Of course he knew. No normal person would really want to sit through that film. They'd have to be bribed with a lot of money. Still, it had served him right—right?

'Let's get something to eat,' he said. 'I'm well aware you're as hungry as I am.'

She'd intended to go home as soon as the movie ended. And frankly she had a headache from tension and hunger. She hesitated.

'You've already cut off your nose to spite your face once tonight,' Ethan said blandly. 'Don't do it again.'

In truth she was so hungry she was beyond able to make a decision now anyway. 'Okay.'

'Great.' He hailed a cab. 'My choice this time. I insist.'

It was a French restaurant. No, it was heaven on earth. Because along one wall stood a gleaming glass case filled with the most amazing pastries—cream cakes, custard and fruit tarts and chocolates. Nadia's functionality reduced even more—she couldn't think or speak, only stare while her mouth watered so much she very nearly drooled. She glanced round the rest of the room and despair hit—the place was packed.

'We won't get a table,' she almost wailed.

Ethan looked down at her, the picture of smug calm in the face of her collapse. 'We already have.'

# CHAPTER FOUR

NADIA nearly fainted with relief. Ethan put his hand on her lower back, pressing her forward to follow the maître d'. She jumped—he had to have one of those trick buzzers in his hand, because he'd just about electrocuted her. The shock made her gulp, and she was hit by a single rational thought. Should she really have agreed to this when her pulse pounded an extra thirty beats per minute the closer the guy got?

Low blood sugar meant she had no choice, right? Those pastries looked too damn good. She glanced back at the display case once more before taking her seat. The sight made her giddy and her thoughts turned crazy again. Maybe she could claim some ground in her quest to intrigue him. Didn't guys like girls who displayed healthy appetites? Wasn't there something seductive if you licked off all the cream or something? If she could raise his want level, drop-kicking him later would have more impact. Hell, yes.

'What do you feel like?' he asked.

She hesitated, toying with some really inappropriate replies—but she figured she should stay subtle at this point to get him over the world's worst movie trick. 'I'm going to skip a main and go straight to dessert. Two desserts, actually, if that's okay?'

His face lit up. 'Sure.'

'What about you?' She mirrored his smile.

He rubbed his flat stomach, 'You don't mind if I do savoury while you do sweet?'

'Not at all.'

Total truce. Or so she'd let it appear. At that point she spent some time studying the menu—purely to have a break from looking at him. Too much of that made her go vacant, and she wanted to stay on track.

'They have an excellent wine selection,' he said blandly. 'Would you like some?'

'Not just at the moment, but you go ahead.' Her smaller physique meant she didn't handle wine that well. She generally had it by the thimble, so she wasn't going to be daft enough to have any now. She waited until the sommelier had left to get the bottle Ethan had selected without even consulting the list. 'So how did you get us this table?'

'I sent a message from the cinema—found out what time the film finished when you were in the little girls' room beforehand.'

She sat back as the waiter poured Ethan's wine, bristling at the phrase "little girl". So he'd known he was in for bum-numbing time at the flicks. She flushed—hating being thwarted, hating feeling this hot. She needed to regain her equilibrium and act more grown-up. She looked at the burgundy liquid. 'Maybe I will have some of that too—thanks.' One glass wouldn't make her legless. And, frankly, she was overheated after that marathon movie and hearing Ethan mutter in French and then spinning her mind by bringing her to gastronomic paradise.

He waited while she sipped. 'Is it okay?'

It was fabulous—smooth, incredibly drinkable and soothing. She sat back after ordering, her happiness skyrocketing at knowing divine food was coming soon.

'Feeling better now?' He looked sly.

'Much, thanks.' She sighed. He smiled, and inside so did she—no doubt he thought that if he added sugar and chocolate he'd have her as gooey as he wanted. He was *so* getting a surprise.

'Did you have a nice night last night?' he asked.

Last night? Oh—that's right. She'd told him she was busy. 'I was catching up with some friends.'

'Yeah, you posted a lot of comments last night.' His smile went evil. 'You live more than half your life online.'

She took another sip of wine to bring her internal thermostat back down. 'You've been snooping.'

'It's not snooping when you put it all out there for anyone to read.'

'And you've been a bit active online yourself,' she said, finally broaching it.

'Ah.' He settled more comfortably in his chair. 'You're mad at me for blogging about our dates?'

'Not mad. Surprised. I didn't think you liked the whole public angle. I thought you wanted to protect your privacy and all that.'

'I'm not the one with contrary privacy issues,' he said pointedly. 'This whole thing isn't actually about you and me, Nadia. Did you think we were going to keep it just between us? What would the point of that be?'

'I'm still not sure what the point of any of this is.'

He chuckled. 'Well, right now, the point is some damn good food.'

With perfect timing the waiter set the dishes down—both her desserts at once, as she'd requested. She pounced, spooning in the sweet. Her nerves scrunched with sensation. Oh, there had to be so much butter in this, so much fine sugar, and put together with so much skill in the kitchen. Edible ecstasy.

He hadn't touched his meal, was just watching her reaction. 'I take it it's nice?'

*'Nice?'* she mini-screeched. 'What kind of a word is *nice*? This is so much better than nice. It's…'

He waited, smile quirking.

'It's indescribable.' She didn't have to fake blatant sensual delight at the dessert. It was genuine and impossible to hide. Frankly, she couldn't get enough of it.

Grinning, he concentrated on his own meal—some meat thing that she really had no interest in. Not when she had the *yum* stuff.

She gave up on trying to converse—not when she had this to concentrate on. She took a bite from each, alternating while panicking about which one she was going to save for the very last bite. The decision was just about impossible. And she was *not* softening towards Ethan in any way whatsoever. She was *not* feeling a ridiculous kind of favour towards him because he'd been clever enough to get them here. She was *not* actually enjoying their conversation and the challenge he embodied.

'What are you thinking about?' he asked eventually. 'You've gone very quiet.'

Well, she couldn't talk when she was so busy inhaling all the cream. But now she was a little sugared up her fighting spirit revived. A divine dessert wasn't going to soften her attitude. 'I'm composing my write-up of this date for my blog.'

Something flickered on his face and he set down his cutlery and pushed his plate away.

'What are *you* going to write about it?' she asked, sweeter than her pastry. 'I'm so looking forward to our next date where you "nail" me.'

'I'm looking forward to that too,' he answered, utterly unabashed.

'My choice for the date, though, isn't it? You wanted to go to the movies for the first.'

'Okay, so what do you want to do?' He conceded surprisingly quickly.

'A day date, I think.' Safe and out in the open, where lots of people would be around. She didn't want to drop-kick him out of touch until the very last date, which meant she was going to have to play the first two just right.

'A *day* date?' Ethan sat back so the waiter could clear their plates.

'Sunday afternoon suit you?' Nadia asked. The sooner it was all over, the better.

'Sure.' He refilled their glasses. 'I'm really looking forward to spending more time with you. You're really good company.'

She suppressed a giggle at his not-quite-hidden sarcasm. Instead she lifted her glass and challenged him. 'I thought you said you weren't going to try to impress me.'

'I guess it's habit.' He shrugged, but let loose that smile.

'You always compliment?'

'Always.' He gazed intently at her. 'And you don't think that's okay.'

'It's not necessarily a bad habit,' she mused. 'But it is if you don't mean what you say.'

'But I do mean it.'

'Always?' She put down her glass and frowned.

'Sure.'

'Really? Don't you sometimes do it because you know it'll make the other person feel good?'

'Is that a bad thing?'

'It is if it's not honest.'

'All right,' he said softly, and leaned across the table. 'You want honesty? Here's some for you—I think you look fantastic in that dress. I think you look really fantastic. I don't want you to. It would be a lot easier if I didn't find you attractive, but *honestly* I think you look…'

'What?'

'It's *indescribable*,' he said roughly. 'Maybe you should feel what you do to me? Can you handle that kind of honesty?'

His hand shot out and grabbed hers, and before she could blink he'd pressed her palm to his chest. Through the cotton she could feel the heat, the fast, rhythmic pounding. Suddenly she could hear it too, thudding in her ears. Her own blood was pumping in time with his. And that wasn't her body's only reaction. She breathed more quickly, shallow. And worst of all was the softening—that warm, melting sensation happening in secret deep inside her. The readying for full possession by a body so much bigger and harder than hers.

She stayed frozen for five seconds too long, until awareness of their surroundings slowly returned. She was stretched across a table in a fine French restaurant, gazing into this guy's gorgeous cinnamon-brown eyes like as if was mesmerised. She was feeling this intense, intimate *thing*…

Then she remembered her rule.

*Don't be too sexual.*

And this was all about the rules. She swallowed, battling to return to the right regime. But every movement was sexual. Everything about him was sexual. *He* was a complete magnet and he knew it. But she was going to disarm him—be the one piece he couldn't pull.

'Oh, you're good,' she said, forcing coolness into her voice, sliding her hand out from under his and bringing it back to press her fist hard against her belly beneath the table-edge. 'You like to have the women want you, don't you? Maybe that's the real reason you compliment so much—it's not their need you're filling, it's your own.'

'And you're really good at coming up with fiction.' He sat back, looking a ton cooler than she'd sounded. 'Whereas I prefer *facts*. And I did my research on you.'

'And what *facts* do you think you found out?' Her temperature soared again as anger bubbled.

'You put it all up there yourself. It wasn't hard to find. That very first entry on WomanBWarned.' He leaned forward. 'Rafe Buxton, wasn't it?'

She avoided answering by taking another sip of her wine, her blood drumming in her ears. How dared he bring that up? That was personal.

'What were you thinking, going with a guy called Rafe in the first place? Weren't the alarm bells ringing then?' he asked, refilling her glass when she set it down.

'I'm not discussing this with you,' she snapped. 'You're unable to feel any empathy. All you want to do is push your agenda.'

'Not true,' he said, annoyingly quietly. 'I only want to understand where you're coming from.'

She just glared at him.

'So he was a "virginity collector"?'

Heat blinded her—anger, yes, but incredible embarrassment too. She'd been so stupid, and she really didn't want to relive it. Didn't want to discuss her pathetic sexual past with such a shark. She didn't want him to know it at all, so she had another sip of wine. A big one.

'So your first was a jerk?' He shrugged. 'You don't have to let it colour the rest of your life.'

Oh, she couldn't not answer that. 'What I won't do is let him get away with it. He preys on young women who are getting their first taste of freedom. Finding independence.' A tutor at a university, he dazzled naïve students with his good-looks and charm and intellectual ability—or at least that façade. Once she'd found out the truth she'd seen that those things were cultivated, not innate or truly deep.

'But we all have to make mistakes. That's part of being human.'

'No,' she disagreed. 'There's a difference between making a mistake and being abused.' And Rafe *had* abused her—and several other young women. 'Illusions shouldn't be shattered like that.'

'But everybody has to face reality some time.'

'You think *that's* reality?' She was appalled. 'So there's no such thing as a committed, loving relationship?'

'Happy ever after?' Ethan shook his head. 'No.'

His cynicism hurt, even though it shouldn't have surprised her. But she could acknowledge a portion of truth in his words regarding that painful episode.

'Maybe not at that age,' she conceded. It had been her second year of university. She'd come from a small northern town and she'd been sheltered. Cosseted, really, by over-protective parents and brothers. As a result she'd been gullible and so easily dazzled. 'I wasn't looking for marriage. But there could have been some kindness and some fun. Not just being another number on his list.' Not being anything but an object. It had been a complete game for him. And once he'd had what he wanted—her virginity—he'd gone on to the next. Another virgin. In the very same week.

Megan.

Only neither of them had known about the other. About all the others.

'You wanted some respect?'

'And honesty.' He'd played them both together. And others. And once they'd found out, by talking at night at a party one night, their friendship had been forged. It was the one truly positive thing to have emerged from an otherwise crushing, humiliating situation. And it had led to WomanBWarned.

'You're really into honesty, huh?' Ethan's brown eyes burned darker.

'There can be nothing without honesty.' Certainly not trust. And without trust or honesty or respect there was nothing to support any kind of a relationship.

'But *you're* not honest.' With careful deliberation he struck at her integrity.

'Yes, I am.'

'No.' He shook his head, a wry smile softening the accusation. 'You're not. You hide behind your website. Behind your stature. All wide eyes—like you're this little thing who has no control over the situations you find yourself in.'

Stunned, she stared at him—he was wrong. 'That's not true.' She hated how people perceived her as weak because she was little. She certainly didn't think she was weak herself. She spent her life proving she wasn't. 'I was tricked,' she said. 'But I admit my own responsibility, my own stupidity.'

'So you won't ever be that stupid again. And you're out to prove it with your website.'

Nadia swallowed more wine to hide the mess of emotion inside her. He made it sound so simple. But there was much more to it. It went so much deeper. She stared down at the stem of her glass and breathed in. The oxygen hit, enhancing the flavour of the wine.

'So tell me about working for Hammond. Is it as great as they all say?' He diverted the conversation, his whole tone lighter.

She didn't lighten to match. Too late she realised he was following his game plan— "get them to share". He thought by inviting her to spill her guts to him she'd actually *like* him for it? Even more wrong.

'It's fine. What about your work? Do you enjoy it?' It was his turn to talk. She'd find his weakness and play on that—his rules.

'It's fine.' He echoed her words dismissively.

She looked up, finding his attention intensely focused on her. She couldn't look away from him. Once more the room receded and there was nothing but his fire-filled deep eyes.

Her senses were swimming now—from the sugar, the warmth, the wine. *Not* the company. She shook her head to clear the confusion.

He broke the intensity, smiling at the waiter and signalling for the bill. 'Time for us to depart.'

The cab ride home passed far more quickly than the one they'd taken earlier. This time she wasn't bothered by the seemingly small space they shared in the back, and there was far less space between them now. She still felt the way his heart had pounded against her palm and her own heart beat faster. Exhilaration, anticipation. Because in moments he'd go for the goodnight kiss and she'd do a quick step to the side. She couldn't wait.

He sat quiet, appearing to be deep in thought. She wondered what about. Hot and half floating, she turned towards him to read his expression better.

He glanced down and smiled.

It was like being tossed into an ice-water bath. Shocked, she blinked and looked again. But her first instinct had read it right—there was none of her desired outcome in his eyes now, none of that heat. Her dress, her wide eyes and smile were having no effect. Despite him saying earlier he thought she looked fantastic in the dress. They'd been meaningless words. Because right now he was clearly more amused by her than attracted. She leaned a little closer as the cab turned a corner, but still nothing. Just benign amusement—and withdrawal. She could *feel* him pulling away.

Why? Where was the move? Where was the "best sex" those women had talked about?

The cab pulled over and Ethan got out, paying him off. He glanced and saw her surprised expression. 'I'll see you to your door and then walk.'

'I'm not inviting you in for coffee,' she said, stupidly hurt by his impersonal politeness.

'I'm not expecting that,' he answered, as if he couldn't care less.

And he couldn't, could he? Anger surged again as she realised this guy was totally not interested. Why not? Why wasn't he, when according to all reports he slayed any female who had the misfortune to slide across his path?

He rested his hand on her back as she turned to walk up her path. Anger burned hotter when she felt again the electric effect that one touch had. His hand was all she could feel. Impotent emotion clogged her throat as she blindly stepped forward.

But because she felt that touch so acutely she felt the stroke of his thumb upwards across her spine—a slow, intimate sweep. The smallest of signals.

Oh, thank goodness—there it was. Satisfaction slammed into her. The man couldn't help himself. Finally he was going to go with some of his moves. She walked slowly now, enjoying the thrill of him moving so close behind her, smiling as she imagined her refusal scene. She'd keep it polite tonight, but playful too—to give him the illusion of possible success in the next date or two.

But in reality it was impossible. For sure.

She unlocked her door and flicked the switch just inside

so light spilled from the room out onto the path. Then she turned to say goodbye, her smile impossible to contain.

He really was very tall up there, still in the shadows, looking down at her. She could tell he was smiling too— but suddenly she knew it wasn't a lust-fuelled smile. It was that amusement again. Was he laughing at her? Her certainty of success faltered.

'Thanks for an interesting evening, Nadia.' Loaded with irony.

He *was* laughing. She'd been wrong about that touch. He wasn't going to do it—no move, no kiss. There was nothing. She felt piqued. And disappointed. And anger swamped her. She was *not* going to let him go without scoring a point of her own.

'I'll see you Sunday,' he said in farewell.

Just before he turned she grabbed a fistful of his shirt and stood on tiptoe as high as she could.

And pressed her mouth to his.

He froze. Didn't pull away, but didn't respond either. So she worked a little harder, stroking his lower lip with her tongue. A faint response then—the smallest flinch of his muscles. But it was so faint she let go and stepped back, suddenly aware she'd made a massive mistake.

'What was that for?' he asked, somehow closer despite her retreat.

'Curiosity,' she flipped back at him, frantically thinking up her defence. She'd crashed out of the floating feeling now. 'I wanted to know if you're as amazing as they all said.'

She felt his muscles firm even more and he loomed closer still.

'And the verdict?'

'Not as hot as I'd been led to believe.'

'But I thought one of your top tips on first dates was not to get too hot.'

'You were playing by my rules?'

'What? You thought you were playing by mine?' He laughed. She could feel the vibrations in the scarce space between them. 'You really have no idea.'

'Don't patronise me.'

'But, darling, you don't just lean in and stick your tongue down a guy's throat.'

Mortification and the hated goosebumps made her skin—and soul—painfully sensitive. So she covered with mock incredulity. 'Are you giving me kissing advice?'

He was a jerk—she hadn't stuck her tongue down his throat and he knew it.

'A little lesson in seduction, if you like.' He stepped even nearer. 'I think you need it.'

She tried to push him away, but he was a mountain in front of her now—immovable and impassable. Her hands were tiny on his chest, her fingers instinctively curling into the fabric of his shirt.

'To begin, Nadia,' he said softly, and with light sarcasm, 'less is more.'

'Is that right?' she snapped, smarting, tipping her chin high to glare into his eyes, deliberately digging her nails into his skin now.

He leaned closer, resting his hands on the wall behind her as he bent, his words whispering across her face. 'Anticipation is everything—didn't you know?'

'It's only everything if the end result is a disappointment,' she said caustically. 'If the end result was as amazing as it's meant to be, then the anticipation would be forgotten in the heat.'

'Oh, you're wrong.' He smiled. 'You need to live moment by moment.' His head lowered. 'It's much more fun.'

He paused, his mouth a millimetre from hers, as he gently instructed, 'You start with lots of soft, teasing touches.'

His lips brushed hers lightly, just once. But the second she went to snap back at him he did it again. Then again and again and again. Until it was lots—as he'd said. Not deep, hungry kisses, but slivers of rich sensuality that made her open her mouth for more before she'd thought to stop it. Then she couldn't think at all—she only wanted to move closer for more.

But he kept them light, lifting back as she tilted towards him.

'Uh-uh,' he teased. 'You keep it the same—don't go deeper until she's begging.'

With one hand he played her like an instrument, gliding one finger after the other across her neck. Not making music but pleasure, with gentle touches. But she *knew* the strength was there.

And she wanted it.

'You keep doing it, keep touching, until she can't think of anything but more, more, more.' He punctuated the words with teasing kisses—now across her jaw and her cheekbones, trailing lazily across her face, until she turned her head to put her mouth back in his path. Because she hadn't been able to think of anything else for eons now.

Vaguely she understood the extent of his charm and experience—he hypnotised with mere words and the most restrained of touches, influencing her mood and her mind and making her want to move. At first she didn't know how to respond. She didn't want to push him away, but something burned. She didn't want to be his mindless plaything. And then she realised he'd told her how to captivate him right back—with soft, teasing touches.

She unfurled her fingers, pressing them lightly on his chest. She felt his flinch as she did so. Through the cotton shirt she could feel his heat. With the tips of her fingers she smoothed slightly downwards, feeling his abs tighten all the more. Then she went north, spreading until she felt his hard nipples. She circled them and began him kissing back—nibbling at his lips, then pressing teensy, saucy smooches across his slightly stubbled jaw.

She realised he'd frozen. One hand was still pressed on the wall behind her, the other still cupped the back of her neck, but his own kisses had stopped.

Fear flashed—he was about to reject her touch again. But then she heard it. In his roughened breathing, in the rigidity of his body, she recognised the strain of holding back.

She smiled, moved her hands the tiniest bit faster, firmer, kissed more feverishly along his jaw. Little kisses, tormenting little touches. Only trouble was she was tormenting herself just as much—she wanted *more*.

He stopped her retaliation by grabbing her hands and forcing them down behind her back. The sudden manoeuvre thrust her breasts into his chest. Sensation shimmered down her body and on pure reflex she arched her spine, pressing closer against him.

His head came down, his mouth crushing hers. Nothing soft and teasing any more. Her neck stretched painfully as he forced her head back and plundered. He thrust his tongue into her mouth, deep and rhythmic. She sucked on it and she felt the growl, felt him tighten even more. With incredible strength he lifted her, sliding her up between his body and the wall—chest to breast, pelvis to pelvis, hand to hand, mouth to mouth.

He didn't thrust against her—just pressed his hips into hers as hard as possible, pinning her so she could feel *all* those inches. Her senses rioted—screaming with over-stimulation while demanding yet more. More skin, more heat. All her instincts were insisting she get closer. She kissed him back as hard and furiously as he kissed her. Rough and hot and reckless. The force of each other's passion merged and grew into something even more powerful between them. Blistering and insane. She shook with the fierceness of her need, aching to cling closer to him. But he still had her hands, so she clung with what she could—her mouth and then her legs. Hooking one around his waist, angling her body so she was more open to his. For a moment it was heaven as she felt him hard against her.

But he tore his mouth away, his hot breath gusting as he groaned, his grip painfully crushing her fingers.

'I'm not going to make it that easy for you, honey,' he said ferociously.

It was torture. It was bliss.

With each ragged breath his chest slammed against her taut nipples.

'I could move this on here and now. Take you to your bed and finish this off. But why the hell should I?' He was furious. 'In the morning you'd be blinded by regrets. You'd convince yourself you'd been used all over again. You'd label me a seducer. Whereas the reality is *you* started this. But *I'm* stopping it.'

Her whole body throbbed, and painfully she lowered her leg from its tight curl around him. She was so sensitised she could feel her blood beating everywhere. He let her go and stepped back. She slid down the wall. She couldn't look up at him. Instead she stared at his hands—bunched into fists at his sides.

'I'm not going to take advantage of a woman who's had one glass of wine too many.'

'I have *not*—' She broke off. Actually, him thinking she was tipsy was the perfect excuse for her incredibly stupid behaviour. Hell, maybe she *was* tipsy. Her head definitely felt cloudy—and her blood was running so quickly in her veins it was dizzying. With only some cake for dinner and then that wine… Yes, that was definitely her problem. And frankly she'd rather he thought she was a cheap drunk rather than this *easy* sober.

Oh, now the regrets poured in. The self-hate. She had been *so* close to being his latest conquest. So damn easy. And he was right, she'd been the one to start it. He hadn't even wanted to start—only she'd pushed his buttons. Deliberately. Because she'd thought she could control it—and him. What a fool she'd been.

He was watching her too closely, knowingly. 'You want to put it down to the wine, Nadia? Would that be convenient for you?'

Oh, it would. But she knew she couldn't. She'd been hot for him from the moment she'd laid eyes on him tonight. And even though she knew he was a jerk she still wanted him. Stupid, *stupid* hormones. 'I'd like you to go now.'

He shook his head. 'You said you were honest. So be honest now and admit that you're attracted to me as much as I am to you.'

She didn't answer. Couldn't. Yeah, here was the most terrible thing: she *was* into him. There was something about him that she really wanted. But this was nothing at all special to him. He hadn't even wanted to kiss her, and only had because she'd started it. Hey, if it was offered on a plate he'd oblige. It was humiliating.

But suddenly he stepped forward, slamming her back against the wall of the house with his big body.

'You know it's true,' he said, low and angry in her ear. 'And now the anticipation is even stronger, right? Because now you know what it's like. How good we'd be.' His head lowered, his lips intoxicatingly close to hers. 'You're going to lie in bed tonight and not sleep a wink because all you'll be able to think about is how much you want me. You'll think about everything you want me to do to you. And what you want to do to me.'

'Yeah, I know *exactly* what I want to do to you.' She tensed and pushed uselessly against his chest. She'd certainly sobered up now. The guy was the most conceited jerk, and she was furious with herself for falling for his façade and his skills—for being pleased that he wanted her when it was no compliment. It wasn't *her* he wanted. It was any woman. It was just that she was the one in front of him now—who'd made it even easier than usual.

'It's not me you should be mad at.' He stepped back, totally misunderstanding her anger. 'Don't forget, Nadia, I've been the perfect gentleman.'

She darted inside and slammed the door, turning the lock with loud, vicious force. Even so, she could hear his chuckle as he walked down the path.

# CHAPTER FIVE

NADIA drank three huge glasses of ice-cold water but was still hotter than a Habanero chilli. Her hands shook as she tossed the glass into the sink and she didn't care when it shattered against the stainless steel. She bent her head and berated herself some more. She was furious. And he'd pay. He'd damn well pay for being such a player.

She stalked to her computer and pulled up the WomanBWarned blog, not stopping to think, just letting the words write themselves.

*So, as you've read over on the Mr 3 Dates and You're Out thread, the man himself has challenged me to go on three dates with him—so he can prove he's not the use-her and lose-her jerk he's portrayed to be. Interesting idea, don't you think? And what does it tell us about the man himself—conceited, much?*

*It's the absolute zenith of arrogance that he thinks he can somehow "win me over" in three dates. He is so cocksure of his attractiveness that he thinks he'll prove what a "nice guy" he really is...*

*But I'm fair, willing to give him the time to try, so I said yes and brought my open mind with me.*

*So let's talk about the first date—he went with the movie idea. As we know, from his new GuysGetWise blog, he's of the opinion that a movie is a good op-*

*tion—despite reading my view that its not the best first date option. Proof that while the guy might say he wants women to "share", he's not actually listening to what we say or want.*

*So I selected a three-hour foreign film that totally sucked. I chose it because he wasn't getting any "chick flick, happy ending hormones" from me. Oh, no. In truth my favourite kind of movie is actually a good thriller or a cut-'em-up horror. I like the adrenalin. But why should he get the benefit from the kind of movie I like? Isn't it up to him to give me the buzz—just from his company?*

*So lesson number one for Mr 3 Dates: you can't stereotype women. We all have different tastes. And guess what? You are not my favourite flavour.*

*Sure, you're good-looking, but is there anything beneath your pretty surface? Not so far as I can tell. Ladies, let me sum up what I learned about him tonight:*

*Mr 3 Dates is the kind of guy who tops up your wine glass when you're not looking.*

*Mr 3 Dates is the kind of guy who thinks a fancy restaurant with beautiful food is all the effort he needs to put in.*

*Mr 3 Dates is the kind of guy who shrugs off any personal questions as if he's afraid he'll reveal something vulnerable that a woman might use "against" him—like the enemy he sees us as. He's all about the hunt and women are the prey.*

*Yes, so far, Mr 3 Dates is totally living up to the rep he's been given online. Without doubt he's a player. The ball's in his court to try prove otherwise. My advice to him?*

*Try harder.*

* * *

Ethan read the blog post that had already appeared by the time he'd power-walked the half-hour home. Not that it had dispelled any of the energy cramping his muscles. He went to the cupboard and poured a whisky, knocking it back neat. It burned. But not as much as what she'd written. What? It was his fault she'd been thirstier than a fish? Not for the wine but for his kisses! She hadn't been able to get enough. But had she admitted that? Hell, no. She couldn't face reality at all—certainly couldn't admit to her own responsibility, her own desires. She'd just warp speeded her way back to Planet Nadia.

Well, he was going to get her to face it even if it killed him. Which it might very well do. Sure, he got what she was saying about her ex. The guy was a total user and an absolute jerk. But Ethan wasn't anything like him. He respected women. And what was so wrong with taking her to a nice restaurant? He totally didn't deserve this—and look how conveniently she'd skipped over half the date, the *important* half. Riled beyond the rational, he opened up his own blog and shredded her right back.

Date Number One *is Done.*
*So Ms **OlderNWiser** went out with me tonight. The Date Movie. Now, all's fair in love and war, and as this is war she'd read my blog. So she said no to the pizza first. And no to the chick flick. Instead she made like she was "desperate" to see one of those arty things with subtitles that goes for hours. To my surprise, I found it not bad, but I suspect it's not her usual thing because she got fidgety. And— oh, look—she's written up the date on her blog already. Yeah, not her usual style. She likes horror? How appropriate.*
*However, as the flick tonight was in French, it*

*was the perfect segue into one of the best restaurants in the city. I'd texted from the cinema and got us a table before the film even started—lesson for you, guys: always be ready to adapt and recover a date that's going sideways. And, for the record, I'd still recommend the chick flick. Horror is for cowards who are too afraid to face their own personal demons, so they try to get the cathartic effect by riding on other people's nightmares.*

*Anyway, the restaurant. From her blog you'd think she wasn't that impressed. Maybe not with me, but the food for sure—she orgasmed her way through two desserts. Or maybe she was faking it, because I suspect her tastebuds can't cope with anything more than bland.*

*Most interestingly, if you go to her What Not To Do on the First Date blogpost, you'll see she has five "don'ts" listed. Guess how many of her own rules she broke tonight, boys?*

*Yeah. You got it.*

*All five.*

*She went to the movies. She drank (and she asked me to fill her glass, by the way). She talked about her ex. She definitely tried too hard—as in tried not to have a good time—but in the end she couldn't resist...*

*Yeah, I know what you're wondering about most— too sexual?*

*Well, if making the first move on the first date makes a woman too sexual, then, yeah, she checked that box too.*

*But let me say this. A gentleman always sees a lady safely home. A gentleman doesn't take advan-*

*tage of a lady's indiscretion. A gentleman doesn't kiss and tell.*

*Ms **OlderNWiser** however—does she tell?*

*Not the truth, it seems.*

*And why is that? Well, why should she, when from the convenient anonymity of her online "user" ID, she can launch her attack? I'm named and shamed while Ms **BitterNTwisted**—sorry, Ms OlderNWiser— hides behind her computer screen in safety. Anyone else see the irony in this? It doesn't seem fair that I and several hundred other guys are named, and yet the women on **WomanBWarned** get to preserve their privacy. Am I going to out her? I know you want me to. But I've made a promise and, contrary to what some may think, I do keep my promises.*

*But I know what else you're wondering. Is Ms **OlderNWiser** actually that old and wise? Truthfully, she's not anywhere near as old as you'd think. Nor is she anywhere near as wise as she claims. So, ladies, I'd be very wary of taking the advice of a woman who's too young to have been even part-way round the block. Just thought I'd point that little truth out for you to think about.*

It took ten minutes for Nadia to read all of Ethan's response, because the red haze in front of her eyes blinded her for most of that time. He was out to undermine her completely, to make her anonymity untenable. This whole situation was untenable. With a vicious tug on the cord she pulled the plug straight out of the wall—not caring about the possible damage she could do to her computer. She turned her back on the black screen and stomped to the shower.

Icy, icy water didn't blast away the fever boiling her

blood. He'd trumped her at every turn. The worst thing was that most of what he'd written was true—she *had* done all those things. Except she hadn't faked it over the dessert—she'd *thought* about doing that to tease him, but she hadn't needed to. And she *hadn't* teased him. He'd been unmoved. But he'd guessed her intent anyway. He'd *known* she'd wanted to snare his interest. And all he'd been was amused—until she'd goaded him into a purely physical response.

And what was the "indiscretion" he hadn't taken advantage of? The wine, or the way she'd made a move on him? Damn it, three minutes in his arms and she'd *wanted* to be taken advantage of—as wholly and hard as he could. She'd basically been begging for it.

*He'd* been the one to stop it and say no. Her stupid plan to be the one woman to say no to him had gone in a flick of his eyelashes.

Angry tears slid down her cheeks. Because now she knew she could never win this war against him. Not when she wanted him as she'd never, ever wanted a man before. Not when she was so out of control she was behaving in a way she'd never behaved before. There was some kind of combustion that occurred within her when he was around—pure aggravation and pure lust. So the only way to combat that was never to see him again. The deal was over—it had to be. Not just for her dignity, but her sanity as well.

She'd take down his thread—much as it galled her. But she had to. Because this humiliation of wanting a guy so badly she was shaking with it was worse than anything.

Ethan lay awake most of the night, reliving the date, thinking about the next, laughing aloud as he imagined her response to his blog. She was going to be furious, and he couldn't wait for her to unleash all her hell on him.

Yes, he'd been attracted from the moment he'd laid eyes on her in her office. But when she'd appeared on her doorstep last night? For the first time in his life he'd been speechless. She'd hassled him over his flattery—but in truth all his usual eloquence had disappeared. There'd been no room in his brain for anything but *wow*. Closely followed by *I want*.

And he'd been honest when he'd told her he didn't want to find her attractive. He really didn't. But he so did. And that attraction was increasing every moment he had with her.

She was completely gorgeous—even when she was hamming it up and looking at him with those doe eyes and biting her lip in total tease fashion. Her enjoyment of those desserts hadn't been faked. She'd totally ignored him and lived in the moment, and he'd enjoyed watching her. He'd really like to watch her in the moments when real pleasure claimed her. He wanted to be the one who made it.

But he'd pulled back. He'd had no choice. He'd been able to tell she wasn't used to much wine. He'd known she'd been drinking more only because he made her uncomfortable—a small fact that he'd take some pleasure in. But he wasn't going to take physical pleasure from a woman whose defences were down. He wasn't going to take advantage. He'd figured she wasn't ready to handle the sparks between them. Not yet. He wasn't sure he was ready yet either.

Only she'd turned his expectations upside down again, hadn't she? She'd kissed him with that hot, slick mouth and the slide of her delicious tongue. He'd almost fallen to his knees, pleading for her to stroke that tongue in some other place. So how could he resist teasing her? A few light kisses to twist up the tension and make the game that snippet more interesting.

Hello, heaven. The rushing in his head? The movement of his body? He'd almost lost control completely and screwed her in her front doorway. It would have been so easy. So good. And over too damn quick.

He wanted a bed, a whole night, and her to be willing and ready and uncomplicated. Yeah, there was the rub. This set-up wasn't anything like his usual flings. Already he knew more about her than he knew about his casual dates. And casual was how he preferred it. He kept things simple—yeah, sexual. And fun. Light and easy and a breezy goodbye.

That wasn't going to be possible with Nadia. It was too late already—how could there be light and easy when there was so much antagonism and mistrust?

But the drive to have her want him—*and admit it*—overrode the alarm bells clanging in the back of his brain. Ms OlderNWiser had passion and energy and he wanted it. Oh, yeah, he wanted to be all over her every which way. He wanted to hear her cry, beg and scream for him. To admit that she wanted exactly what he wanted and every bit as badly. Because there'd never been a want as bad as this in all his life, and he was not going to let her deny it.

Early in the morning he rolled out of bed, completely unrefreshed, took a freezing shower to try and wilt the raging erection he'd been crippled with the last twelve or so hours, then went to work and tried to concentrate. But it, like his body, was too hard.

Finally he picked up the phone. He'd watched the comments appear—yeah, some of his cruder team-mates were getting vocal now. He drew a deep breath, discomfort niggling over some of the things they were suggesting he do. Well, he wasn't uncomfortable with the suggestions themselves—hey, he'd been thinking those exact same things and several hundred more—but he didn't like it being out in the public like this. Another comment pinged up— really crass. He turned away from the screen as he waited for her to answer, damn glad her real name wasn't out there in the blogosphere.

'Hammond Insurance. Nadia speaking.'

His fingers clamped the phone harder, responding to that hint of ruthlessness in her voice. The tough lady tone hinted at the tiger within.

'Good morning.' He didn't give his name—knew he didn't need to. She was as alert to him as he was to her.

Yeah—all he got was silence.

'How's your head?' He decided to provoke her. He had a nagging pain in his—a nagging that drilled down the rest of his body too, because it still resented the way he'd ripped away from her last night.

'I'm not going out with you again. The deal's off.'

He'd expected it, but even so her words winched his stiff muscles even tighter. 'You're such a coward,' he said softly.

'No, this is just a waste of time.' She sounded crisp. 'You're everything those women said and then some.'

'Not true.' He sat back in his seat, smiling at her illogicality and her determination to resist the challenge. 'If I was really a user I'd have taken everything you offered last night. And be honest, Nadia, you offered *everything*. But instead I was chivalry incarnate. Shouldn't I get recognition for that?'

'You're the devil incarnate,' she snapped, the ice barely covering her volcanic reaction. 'This whole thing is over.'

'So you're going to identify yourself? You're going to pull your forum?'

'I'll pull your thread. You can do whatever you want. I don't care.'

'You'll risk your job?' He frowned. Was she really going to give in so easily? That didn't sound right. And it was exactly what he didn't want. No way did he want this battle to be over—not now it was getting so interesting.

'Is your thirst for revenge so great you'd see me on the street?'

Ethan tensed. She was calling his bluff—and, no, he wouldn't expose her. He didn't want her to lose her job. He needed some other kind of leverage. Fortunately he figured he had it. 'But you care about your site.' He clicked his computer to refresh the screen. 'Haven't you seen the number of hits on my little blog this morning? And all the comments on yours?'

Nadia buried her head in her hand, closing her eyes, wishing she could close her ears to his charismatic voice— she couldn't halt the response in her bones to the smile she could *hear*.

'Nadia?'

She pressed the phone closer to her ear and sank lower into her seat. Just the way he said her name made her wet. Maybe it was some kind of hormone imbalance or something? Maybe it was because she hadn't had a date or sex or anything remotely romantic for so long? Maybe she'd subconsciously fixated on that one bit of his reputation— the "best sex ever" bit? Okay, not even subconsciously— it was right up there in the forefront of her brain, flashing neon-sign-style.

'Have you seen them?' he asked again.

'No.' For the first time in years she hadn't checked her computer on waking. And now she was at work. The only people in the company who had access to social networking sites on their computers were those in Human Resources, so they could check the online presence of employees and possible recruits—yes, they checked the profiles of applicants, and their posts. They didn't hire people who made fools of themselves or who had loose lips. That meant she could check his page now. She glanced behind her—no one could see her screen. Super-quick she typed in the URL. It only took a moment to load. She gasped— there were over a hundred comments. She read the first few and her lungs froze.

'Isn't that why you run your site, Nadia? To feel important? To be popular? Don't you *want* to get all these hits and all these comments? Isn't this the whole point?'

No, it wasn't. And there were hits and there were *hits*. And there were some really awful hits on there. Personal, derogatory, mortifying comments. As she loaded the second page to read more, another couple were added. She read them. They were getting worse. Nadia's eyes stung and she tried to blink the acid away.

'I hate you for this.' She couldn't keep the emotion out of her voice.

'Doesn't feel nice, does it?' he said, in his hatefully compelling voice.

'You should be moderating the comments.'

'Like you moderate the lies on *your* website?' He chuckled. 'Surely this is the best thing ever? All this extra traffic making the world more aware of your site.'

Nadia didn't answer. She flicked to WomanBWarned and saw the number of comments there—with much nicer, "go-girl", supportive words. She breathed out—they were good, and her hit rate was incredible.

'So it's not over, is it, Nadia?' Ethan purred. 'I don't think there's any going back now. And I'm really looking forward to whatever it is you have planned for our day date.'

Was he, now? Nadia grinned, her confidence and courage streaming back after the "we love your blog" and "take him down" boosts.

'I really don't want another date with you,' she said, lying to them both.

She went back to his blog post and added a comment beneath all the phnaar, phnaar macho innuendo—

*Typical boys, you can only think south of the belt buckle.*

'You know you don't have a choice. You know you can't resist.'

Her hand froze on the mouse, because he was right and she couldn't think straight. 'In three days' time I'll wake at four in the morning with the perfect plan to take you down eighty pegs.'

'And for now?'

'Kiss my ass.'

'Ask me nicely and I might oblige.'

Nadia responded the only way she could think of. She hung up.

# CHAPTER SIX

**WomanBWarned:**
*Progressing to second & third dates...*

*The day date is the perfect way to get to know each other without the pressure of romantic expectations that can be present in the evening. So it's a good option for early on in your dating relationship. Suggestions for fun day dates:*

*A picnic in the park*

*A walk in the local botanic gardens or zoo*

*Visiting an art gallery*

*Beachcombing*

*Something adventurous—paddling a canoe in the park, paintball if you're that way inclined.*

*But here's a tip—don't choose something that one or other of you is an expert at if the other is a complete novice. No one likes to look a fool.*

*Also, while it's nice to be getting to know each other, and it's understandable to want to see if he'll integrate well with your friends, go easy. It can be intimidating to be introduced to a ton of strangers who are all sizing you up. And definitely don't introduce him to your family too soon!*

\* \* \*

ETHAN studied the list and wondered which of those things she was going to inflict on him on Sunday. Actually, he thought it was a damn good idea. The cold light of day would be the perfect place for her to face some undeniable truths—like the sizzle between them. There'd be no wine for her to hide behind.

He sighed and brought up his own stupid blog. He had to write a post, but honestly he didn't know what he was going to say. The number of comments had gone up massively and he felt a buzz. Yeah, he could see the attraction now—it was somehow satisfying to see more and more people were tuning in to his words. Good grief, was he going to turn as narcissistic and ratings-driven as his dad? Uh—no. Because he was about to write himself into a corner.

He typed a title.

*Nailing Her on Number 2*

Now what? How the hell was he going to get around this one?

*Have to be careful here, boys, because as we know **OlderNWiser** is reading my write-ups—and commenting now too. Welcome, darling—we always appreciate your thoughts. But it means I can't give away too much strategy before the deal.*

Actually, he didn't have any strategy. He was winging it now—going on his gut in these uncharted waters.

*What I can tell you is that date number two is the lady's choice and she's opted for a "day date"—I think this is her thinking she'll escape the nailing.*

*But I guess that depends on what it is you all think
I'll be nailing.*

*I may be a bloke, but I'm not that crude. Not always.*

Yeah, right. It was all he could think about. All he wanted,
wanted, wanted.

*What I'm talking about here is not the physical, I'm
talking the emotional. The intent. What you want
to nail on date number two is her interest. Get her
intrigued and soon enough you'll get anything else
you might care to want.*

*So how do you nail her interest?*

*You tease out her curiosity, and with that you trap
her. Tease and trap, boys. Give them a little mystery,
a little reticent man, and then let them think they can
be the one to figure you out...*

Ethan had been right. Nadia couldn't sleep. Couldn't stop
thinking about him and her and what she shouldn't do with
him if she were going to remain a sane, sensible woman.
But she wanted to, and in just a few short days it had become a complete obsession.

Yeah, she knew she was obsessive—she got these great
ideas and ran after them with all her energy. Some ideas
were great—some were rubbish. Ethan Rush wasn't a great
idea. Did she really want to risk herself with him? She
leaned back in her big comfy chair and stared at his taunt-
ing words on the screen while the ones he'd whispered to
her replayed round and round in her head—that she should
live *moment by moment* and not be a *coward*. And on top
of that temptation he planned to "tease and trap" her? Oh,
he already had. She was so interested already. He had all
the benefit of his beautiful body and the charm that he'd

honed with years of experience. And he was clearly smart. Very smart. She liked that in a guy too. But she snorted at the last line—she didn't want to figure him out. She just wanted to jump his bones.

Only she *was* being a coward. For what was the risk here? What was it she was so afraid of? A broken heart? She laughed at the ridiculousness—there was no way her heart was at risk with Ethan Rush.

Suddenly she saw she'd been thinking about this all the wrong way. Full of fear about being used, hating herself for coming so close to being just another of his easy conquests. She didn't want to be the passive victim.

So then she shouldn't be passive, right? She should be the one in charge. She should do what she wanted to do—control the situation and her response to it. Sure—live in the "moment", be brave, be the boss.

This wasn't just about the notches on his bedpost—what about her own bedpost? Why shouldn't she carve in a beautiful mark to remind her of an incredible sensual experience? Why shouldn't she enjoy the rush that was Ethan?

She wanted, and there was nothing wrong with wanting.

And he wasn't completely indifferent. Yes, his response had been instinctive—she knew that. The guy had a high sex-drive. That was okay—because for sure they weren't talking relationship. They were talking hook-up. She just had to be sure she understood what it was she wanted.

Rafe's intentions had not been honourable. She'd been expecting something different from that relationship. She'd wanted more. She didn't want more from Ethan. She just wanted his body, his expertise, to feel some more of the way he'd made her feel.

Wasn't she worth it? Didn't she deserve to experience that kind of sizzling animal passion? Why couldn't *she* use instead of being the one who was used? It wasn't as if it was ever going to bother him. He wasn't sensitive enough to get hurt. If she let go of her old 'happy ever after" expectation and just went with "what feels right now" she'd be fine.

She giggled at her thoughts, mocking the way her brain could work, twisting and turning to justify something simply because she wanted it so badly. But she deserved some fun and he'd be good. And then it would be over—this bubble of obsession would be burst.

But what of her original aim? Could she still teach him a lesson? She was under no illusions that he'd fall for her if she slept with him, but surely she could still execute a flick-off somehow? She'd figure something out…

The immediate problem was that he was resisting the heat between them. Even though she knew he'd been turned on the other night, he'd stopped. She was going to have to subvert his mission to prove himself a nice date. She was going to have to make his physical instincts overrule his intellectual intentions.

She was going to have to provoke him into action.

Saturday morning Ethan snatched up his phone when he read the caller display. 'Hello, darling. Ready to do date two?'

'I might be ready by tomorrow. Can you wait that long?'

Ethan's brows shot up. So did another part of him. He hadn't expected her to purr quite like that. He stretched back in his bed and enjoyed listening as she continued softly.

'I've checked the forecast and it looks good. So we can meet there.'

'Where?' he asked.

'Hyde Park. By the Serpentine.'

'Going public?' he noted.

'And in broad daylight.'

He could hear the smile in her voice. It made him smile all over.

'Coward,' he mocked.

'Not at all. But…' Her voice trailed. 'You need to dress for action.'

'What kind of action?' He couldn't suppress his physical reaction to the way she'd tossed out that little *double entendre* so carelessly.

'Something you can move in.'

'Okay.' He couldn't move for the anticipation making him rigid now. He tossed the phone away and breathed deep to relax. Hell, he had to get out of bed and do something to release some energy. She was definitely taking him for a walk in the park, like on her list—too damn tame. But perhaps that was her point.

The next afternoon couldn't come soon enough for Ethan. He forced himself to walk rather than run there. The sun beat hot on his back and people were at the park in their masses. Ice-cream vendors were doing a roaring trade. He wanted them all to clear off. He wanted to be alone with her.

He loitered by the water, on edge, wondering if she was going to stand him up. His edges sharpened. If she did, he was damn well going to make her pay—somehow.

A roaring sound behind him grew louder, and just as he turned something crashed into him. A lithe body. A very hot one. His hands automatically shot out to steady her.

She blinked and smiled up at him. 'Sorry I'm late.'

He kept his hands on her narrow waist. 'Not a problem.'

She was taller. He glanced down. She was wearing rollerblades. Oh, man. A sexy roller-chick image flashed in his head. He blinked it away and checked out the reality.

Nope—not minuscule hotpants, but black leggings and a tee shirt.

Good grief—she was wearing exercise clothes. Workout gear to a date. She'd meant that kind of action.

'Thanks for making such an effort,' he said drily. 'This is what you have planned for us?' Fricking rollerblading round the park? He really didn't think so.

She looked coy. 'Aren't you game?'

'Weeeeell…' he drawled, deliberately keeping hold of her. 'According to your website you shouldn't do something on a day date if one person is an expert at and the other is a novice.' He was not putting on any damn skates.

'But you told me I shouldn't live my life by all those rules.' She did her wide-eyed innocent look. 'I'm just taking your advice.'

'You're being a bitch.'

Her smile blossomed. 'Or is it that you're a coward?'

He let her go then, and stalked over to a cart where there was a guy renting out skates. Nadia, of course, had her own—not the ancient, shonky-looking ones the rental dude had displayed. Ethan glanced at her. Her feet were so small that even in the ridiculous boots with wheels on they still looked tiny. Whereas *he'd* be doing a Bigfoot impersonation. But then he checked over the rentals again and gave a muttered word of thanks before turning to her, totally satisfied. 'Sadly they don't have skates in my size.'

'He has skates in all sizes.' Nadia pushed past him to check out the range.

'I have big feet.'

She turned and looked down at his feet. He watched the pink deepening in her cheeks as she looked—*slowly*—back up his body. He knew she was wondering whether another body part measured up.

Of course it did.

'Oh.' She looked flustered. 'Um…so what do you want to do?'

Ethan grinned. He knew exactly what he wanted to do—but he wasn't going to. 'My flat isn't far. I have a bike there. We could grab it and come back. You skate—I bike. Then we can get an ice-cream and sit on the grass, yeah?'

She shrugged. 'Okay, that sounds like a plan.'

Ethan strode out while she skated just in front of him, circling back when she got too far ahead. Actually, her exercise gear was growing on him. He liked watching the slide of her thighs as she took each stroke. The leggings and little tee emphasised her compact body and cute butt. She was slim, but still had curves. He liked the light flush building in her cheeks—it made her eyes sparkle more than ever.

'You skate a lot?' he asked.

'I skate to work every day.'

'What?' He stopped on the footpath and waited for her to come back to him. 'To *work*?'

'Yeah.' She looked surprised at his amazement. 'And home every night. It's only forty minutes each way.'

'In the filthy London traffic and across the middle of Hyde Park? What time do you go in the morning?'

'I don't know. Seven or so. Shower and change at work. Have breakfast at my desk. It works well.'

'All year—in *winter*?'

'Well, not if it's raining.'

'But it's dark and you're alone. Or do you have a skate buddy or something?'

She looked at him as if he was mad. He *was* mad. 'No skate buddy.'

'You shouldn't do it.' Some primal feeling had built in him. 'It's not safe.'

'Oh, please—you think it's dangerous?'

'It *is* dangerous. The park is big. Any weirdo or creep could drag you off, and that would be that.'

'Here's the thing, Ethan.' She skated up to him. 'When I'm on wheels, I'm *fast*.'

'Oh, really?' He *wasn't* being distracted by her flirting.

'You know, in my experience—'

'Vast as it is,' he interpolated sarcastically.

'Yes.' She sent him a slayer look. 'There are two kinds of men—protective and predatory. I'd never have expected you to step into the former category.' She put a light hand on his chest. 'I don't need a protector, Ethan.'

'You want to be hunted?' His attempt to ignore the flirt failed. 'Are you sure that's what you want?'

'Well, I definitely don't need someone who thinks a little thing like me shouldn't wander down the main road without a bodyguard.'

'Because you can take care of yourself?' He folded his arms across his chest to hide how tense she had him, and looked down at her the way he knew she hated.

'That's right,' she purred, but he knew her claws were out.

He smiled. Oh, she was begging to be taught a lesson. 'You really think you could get away from a guy like me— if I set my mind to it.'

'Absolutely.'

'Prove it, then. Let me get twenty paces ahead, and then you try and skate by me. Let's see if you're really fast enough.'

Excitement kindled in her eyes, turning the emerald jewels into bright, liquid fire. 'All right, then. You go ahead.'

He walked backwards so he didn't break eye contact as he moved away from her. She waited, hands on hips in total defiance, as he stepped further away. But she had no idea what she was in for. He'd been on the first fifteen at school and at university. He knew how to tackle.

Twenty paces out, he turned away from her, every sense attuned. His hearing was especially acute, waiting for the rhythmic sound of her skates on the concrete. There it was—the strikes getting faster and louder as she neared. He stepped up his own pace, breaking into a run. As she drew abreast of him he put on an extra burst of speed.

He wasn't stupid—this was a narrow stretch of path and she had to stay on the smooth surface to maintain her speed. So he blockaded—pushing her nearer the edge as she tried to pass. And just as her energy spurted he scooped one arm around her waist, half lifting her as he ran that bit faster, further to the side, until they both fell to the grass. Full body tackle. Relentless in his pursuit, he rolled so he was on top of her, clamping her arm between their bodies, completely stopping her escape. He cupped one hand over her mouth and held down her free arm with the other while he adjusted his position to trap her legs between his.

She shivered violently beneath him. His muscles locked tighter in response.

'Gotcha,' he ground out through teeth clenched in masculine victory. 'No one's come to your rescue, Nadia.' His words slurred as all his predatory instincts celebrated, shutting down his brain and firing up his body. He kept his hand over her mouth. Tried not to enjoy having her at his mercy too much. But he failed on that one.

Beneath his tense bicep, her breasts rose and fell quickly.

'It's the middle of the damn day and you're mine to do what I want with. In the morning, when you skate through here, there are even fewer passers-by. You'd have no chance.'

He felt the ripple in her body again, watched the green in her eyes deepen, some emotion welling up in her. But it wasn't fear.

Oh, hell.

It swamped him too, obliterating all those intentions. He tried to hold on…meaning to prove that point. But he couldn't remember what the point had been now… He knew what he wanted, but he was not going to—not going to…

He lifted his hand and quickly kissed her—hard.

And he groaned as quick became long and slow. He dived into the sensations—the hungry, soft mouth, the sweet slide of her tongue. His brain shut down completely as he was immersed in searing, delicious heat. For ever and a bit later he lifted his head and looked at her. Her tee had rucked up a bit when he'd tumbled her down, baring her midriff. Now he ran a single finger just above the snug waistband of her black leggings, loving the satin feel of her smooth warm skin. Loving the catch of her breath even more.

He watched her reaction—the increase in her pulse, the liquidity of her eyes—and went bolder still, firmly pressing the palm of his hand against her belly, feeling the response ripple through her. Oh, man, she had fire.

He slid his hand beneath that waistband and watched her mouth open in a silent *oh*. For a brief moment her eyes closed as he went lower, brazenly sliding his fingers right down into her pants.

Her whole body spasmed.

He paused, breathing hard as he felt her instinctive rocking up to meet his hand. She wanted him.

'Don't be too pleased with yourself,' she panted, defiant to the end. 'I'm always hot after I exercise.'

'Oh, very hot.' He delved deeper. Slow, exploratory

strokes that he quickened when he felt how incredibly hot she was. Hot and wet and uncontrollably arching her hips to ride his touch.

She shrugged, but she had that drugged look. 'It makes me more orgasmic.'

*Ooooookay.* 'My touching you?' He leaned closer to catch her breathless whisper.

'No...'

'No?' He half laughed, half groaned as he massaged her wet heat, sliding his fingers deep and thumbing her sweet spot. 'How close are you?'

'Not...that close.'

He barely caught her answer she was so breathless. Ethan exulted in the fire escalating within her, flicked his fingers that bit faster. And incredibly, awesomely, that was all it took.

Her head arched back violently, her eyes closing as she clamped hot and tight, suddenly releasing hard and fast, a strangled moan slipping from her full lips.

'Did you just come?' Astounded, he had to ask to be sure. 'I hardly did anything.'

And he was so excited he was about to make a fool of himself.

'Like I said,' she panted, opening her eyes—they glittered so bright they revealed nothing. 'Exercise makes me more orgasmic. You know—the blood was already pumping.'

Oh, he wanted pumping. He wanted pumping right now. Only he was stuck in the middle of a public park and he had no chance of getting what he wanted in the next five minutes. His jaw ached because his teeth were clenched so hard. But he had to clarify her outrageous statement. 'So you're saying it wasn't really me? That it was the *exercise*?'

Her shoulders lifted lazily.

He laughed, delighted with the appearance of her inner ball-breaker. She was totally angling to emasculate him. 'So five minutes of skating got you to screaming point? Wow. That's a good tip to know. You meant it when you said the wheels made you fast.'

All he could see were green jewel eyes, a lazy smile and lightly flushed cheeks. She even let out a little sigh of satisfaction as she muttered, 'Yes.'

Oh, he didn't believe her. He focused, reading every tiny little sign. Understanding her was suddenly everything. Her tongue flicked, quickly dampening the corner of her mouth. She lowered her lashes, hiding her dawning reaction.

Unadulterated challenge and nothing but.

Reluctantly he slid his fingers from their newfound favourite home and lifted them to his lips. He leaned over her, pressing his aching erection right between her upper thighs, not caring if he squashed her for this one second—to get his point across.

Her eyes widened, glazing over again, her breathing hitching to almost hysterical. Yeah, she liked it. And he loved how much she liked it.

'You think you're going to teach me a lesson?' he taunted softly. 'Trouble is, you're not satisfied yet, darling. You and I both know that was just the warm-up.'

# CHAPTER SEVEN

NADIA didn't know what she wanted first, second or third. It was worse than when she hadn't eaten for a few hours. Decision-making was completely beyond her. So was prioritising. She didn't want to move, but she was desperate to. She didn't want Ethan to lift his gloriously heavy body from hers, but she wanted him to hurry so they could get somewhere private. She wanted him to go on top, go underneath, go down. She wanted him so many ways she couldn't think, breathe or speak for the anticipation.

Yes, now she knew just how good the guy was. Some of it was the packaging, some of it was chemical, but most of it was attitude and skill. He had every right to be the cocksure dude he was. And which was more important to Nadia right now—deflating his ego or having the time of her life?

Time of her life. Hands down.

Maybe he felt it—the moment of pure surrender, the subtle relaxation of her body as she gave in. Maybe the desperation was all too obvious in her expression. But he smiled and lifted away from her. Maintaining blatant, blistering eye contact as he extended a hand to haul her up.

She awkwardly walked the few paces across the grass to get back to the path, her thighs so wobbly she doubted she could skate any more. But some kind of muscle memory locked in. Some last shred of dignity—the need to mask how completely shattered she'd been by those few moments in the grass and pretend some more it had all just been the exercise. As she began to recover a little co-ordination he started to jog. She skated faster to keep up.

'We'll continue with the plan and go get my bike,' he said, sounding too damn unruffled and making her doubt everything again—especially that hungry stare he'd subjected her to as he'd pressed her into the grass.

She concentrated hard on the concrete path, not wanting him to see how disappointing his words were. She was gutted that they hadn't done everything right there and then. Had he recovered his reason now? Was he going to go back to being the gentleman—not the rogue who always took what he wanted without giving a damn?

She really wanted him to take what he wanted. She wanted to *be* what he wanted. She skated as her energy returned to comic book superhero levels—courtesy of frustration. As she sped up, so did he, until they were moving swiftly out of the park, down the paths, easily avoiding the pedestrians—as if they really did have some kind of superhuman co-ordination and speed.

She glanced at him, absorbed the effortless grace of his big body in motion. He was fit—surprisingly fast for someone so tall. And maybe it wasn't so effortless—because as she looked closer she saw his fists clenched so tight his knuckles were white, his big biceps more defined than ever. Anticipation sent adrenalin licking through her veins again.

His hand suddenly closed on her upper arm, and he gave a sharp tug so she veered off course, spinning in a half-circle and colliding against him. His other hand caught her round the waist, pressing her chest and belly to his and keeping her there.

'We're here.' He lifted her, keeping her clamped to him,

and jogged up the three steps to the main door, wincing as
the toe of her boot accidentally connected with his shin.
She was too puffed, too turned on, to apologise. At the
top he lowered her, releasing her arm to reach behind her.
His other hand kept her pushed hard into his hot body. She
heard a series of beeps, figured he'd pushed a security code
into the pad next to the big door. Sure enough, she heard
a click as it unlocked.

'Can you manage the carpet with your skates?' He
didn't wait for an answer, just pushed her so she rolled
in backwards.

The door slammed shut behind him.

He stopped on the first-floor landing and pulled out
a key. 'Hot again after that exercise?' he asked, dripping
with innuendo.

Oh, yeah—as if it was the exercise warming her up.
What a liar she was. She'd been hot for days, since that
kiss after the movies. It was *all* him. But while she wasn't
about to deflate his ego this minute, she wasn't going to
puff it up even more either.

'Not hot enough,' she said bluntly, and slid past him
onto the wooden floor of his apartment, gliding down the
hall and into the main room. It was a big apartment—taste-
ful. Not that she took in many details.

She heard the door shut and his fast pace. His hands
caught her hips and drew her back against him, his mouth
hot on the side of her neck. She instantly angled her head
so he could access more skin. Her skates propelled her
forward, away.

He growled as he pulled her back against him and
nudged his leg between hers. 'It's like a teen fantasy. Your
legs literally slide apart.'

For him they did. They would even without the wheels.
He shaped her body, cupping her breasts and then slid-

ing down her stomach. She loved the size and firmness of his hands. Her breathing escalated—fast, shallow—and she shamelessly leaned back against him, encouraging him to continue the hot trail of kisses over her skin.

'I wasn't going to do this,' he muttered, furiously nuzzling into her neck.

'You could always stop,' she taunted, pressing her butt harder against his erection.

'You know that's not possible.' He groaned, gliding hard and firm down the length of her body, pressing pleasure into her skin and deeper into her muscles. 'You sure you can handle the hurt?' he asked roughly.

'Is there going to be hurt?'

'I didn't think there was usually. But people have been at pains to point out to me that I'm wrong on that. So I think it's only fair to warn you.'

Amused by his flash of conscience, she teased him some more with her body. 'Who's to say it'll be me who feels the hurt?'

'You're the one with the venomous website.'

'I've already been warned, Ethan. Don't worry.'

He lifted the hem of her tee shirt and she instantly lifted her arms to let him take it right off. But as he released his hold on her she glided forward again.

He swore in annoyance and then simply pushed her forward some more, until she crashed into the back of a leather armchair. Her feet couldn't move further forward now—and he was in place firmly behind her. She bent at the waist so she could feel his hard length pressing closer to her core. She reached into the cup of her bra and pulled out the condom she'd hidden there, passed it back to him.

He grunted. 'A woman who knows what she wants. Full of surprises, aren't you?'

With barely leashed ferocity he undid her bra and held

each strap in his hands—using it like a bridle to control how far she could lean to and from him.

And she wanted to be ridden. 'Harder,' she moaned, thrills shivering along every vein.

He pulled tighter, flattening her breasts against the cotton, her nipples sensitive against the material. He teased with his hips. Round and round, pressing hard and close and then away again, while he kissed from across from one shoulder to the next, stopping to nibble at her neck and her upper back. Her breathing shortened, keeping rhythm with the circling motion of his pelvis against her. She was going to come again, and he was still fully clothed.

Not okay. She wanted him inside her.

She rocked harder, faster, circling her hips back against him, wanting to stir him beyond restraint so they'd strip and screw right now—now, *now*. Suddenly he picked her up and started walking across the lounge back towards the hall. She struggled so much he dropped her, and her feet went out from under her. She crashed onto her hands and butt.

'What's wrong?' He thudded to his knees beside her.

'I don't want to see the notches on your bed.' She scrambled to get on all fours. 'I'd rather be out here on the floor.'

'I haven't slept with nearly as many women as you seem to think,' he spat back, equally furious, his hand shooting out to grasp her wrist. 'And so what, anyway? Isn't it now that matters? I'm not sleeping with anyone else right now. I'm *not* going to do that to you.'

'I still don't want to see your room,' she growled. 'I just want to…to…' Her lungs jerked so hard she could hardly speak.

'You just want a quick shag—is that it?'

'Now,' she said bluntly.

'Well, we're getting rid of the skates first.'

'Fine.'

He fought with one while she worked on the other, until with heavy thuds he tossed them both over his shoulder and in one smooth movement pulled her beneath him as he rolled over her. She liked that he was fearless about being on top of her. She liked how much he weighed her down.

'That's what you want, isn't it?' He grinned evilly down at her. 'Like to be dominated, darling?'

'Watch your step, Ethan. You're more vulnerable that you realise.'

'You think?'

She ran a nail down the side of his neck while she slipped her other hand between them. She cupped his balls though his shorts and squeezed ever so slightly. He flinched and rose on all fours astride her, suddenly smiling—even though she knew he was as angry at her as he was turned on.

He yanked the dangling bra free from her body and then with two hands pulled her black leggings down, revealing her knickers.

He slid them halfway down her body and stared at the plain white panties.

'Cotton Lycra.' She tried not to sound too apologetic. 'Comfortable for exercise.'

'Indeed,' he said. 'And nice and stretchy.' He grasped them, pulling them to the side, and very gently blew warm air over her. 'Something very tantalising about it.' He let the material cover her again and pressed his open mouth against the cotton.

She'd just about burst out of her skin at the luscious breath, and now the wet heat of him through the cotton was absolute torture.

'Damn it, Ethan,' she groaned. 'You make me mad. You make me laugh.' She banged her head back on the floor, arching as he licked her through the cotton. 'You drive me crazy.'

'Well, that's totally fair.' He switched to sucking and twisting his tongue into the cotton. 'You do the same to me.'

She shook her head frantically. But it didn't matter now—too late. She cried out through clenched teeth and contracting muscles as she came again.

She opened her eyes to see Ethan's satisfied smile as he stripped the last of her clothes from her body and then stripped himself. He dealt with the condom and then looked up, his brows flickering when he saw she was watching avidly.

'What shall we do now?' he asked innocently.

'I've orgasmed twice already,' she said bluntly. 'I just want you.'

He hesitated. She could feel his tension as this time he carefully took the bulk of his weight on his elbows. He gently probed her with his thick erection.

She shivered, all the goosebumps back. 'Girth is good, Ethan.'

He laughed and kissed her. 'You could use that as another website. GirthIsGood.'

'Yeah?' She rocked sinuously beneath him, wanting him to close those last few inches. 'I've got a better one.'

'Mmm?' He kept up the tease, still not penetrating.

'Pump. Now. Please.'

'Okay.' But still he didn't. Instead he bent and with a wide mouth sucked hard at her nipple while stroking with his tongue, his hand cupping its twin so it didn't feel neglected. Something else felt neglected.

Breathlessly she tightened her grip on him, jerking him up by the hair. 'Do me or die,' she ordered.

'Oh, that's nice.'

But she'd won. She saw the flare of his nostrils, the narrowing of his gaze as his focus centred.

He pushed forward. Hard.

She moaned—a low, wild sound that came from deep in her chest—and he paused. She could feel his heart thumping. She inhaled deep, then sighed and smiled. 'Good, good, good,' she muttered. 'Now give me more.'

'Demanding,' he choked. 'So demanding.'

'You like it.'

'I do.'

'So why have you stopped?'

'I like it too much.'

'Ethan...'

'Will you give me a break?' he snapped. 'I move an inch now and I'll come, and I don't want to come just yet. I don't want this to be over that soon.' He exhaled sharply, closed his eyes on her, his whole expression creasing into a frown of agony and need, frustration and determination.

'Oh...' She all but came again herself. Thrilled. She didn't want it to end yet either, but she wanted him to feel as ecstatic as her—as desperate.

'It's not funny.' He moved out of her.

'What are you doing?' She growled her disappointment.

He frowned right back at her. 'It's okay for you to be fast. It's not okay for me to be fast,' he gritted. 'I don't want either of us to end up frustrated.'

He sat back and rearranged her, pushing her legs further apart, and then moved forward again, stopping to suck her some more before sliding his length deep inside and causing those mini-convulsions in her again.

'How hard?' he asked, the strain audible.

'Rough as you can.'

'Oh—' He swore crudely and swiftly left her again, rising to his knees and rubbing his hands over his face as he inhaled huge gulps of air.

She sat up and stared, amazed to see him struggling so much. 'Are you worried about your reputation, Ethan?'

Didn't he know he'd already given her the best sexual experience of her life? Or did he think she had orgasms in public parks every day of the week?

'No.' He glared at her. 'But I'm not completely in control of myself with you.'

'And you usually are?'

He grunted.

She smiled, crazily pleased that he was having a hard time coping with how turned on he was. 'Well, I don't care about control,' she said quietly. 'I just want you inside me.'

'What you say to me,' he said through even more tightly clenched teeth, 'does not help.'

'You want me to shut up?'

He looked at her for a long time and then suddenly smiled, the tension in his face altering from strained to wicked—but still edgy. Had he won whatever battle it was he was having with himself? 'Yeah—why don't you just come and take what you want?'

'All right.' She rose to her knees and crawled the half-metre to sit astride him.

He lifted his face to look her in the eye. She saw the mix of molten fury and desire as she rocked herself over the tip of his erection a few times. She'd known it would be good, but she hadn't expected this kind of blistering, on-the-edge passion. Equal parts anger and hunger and helpless humour.

She put her hands on his shoulders, her fingers spread wide, but still not big enough to curl right around them. That didn't matter. She could use them as leverage anyway. And she pushed down hard as she took him in to his hilt.

His hands were pressed hard into the floor, and she pushed harder on him as she lifted her hips and ground back down. The sensation was outrageously awesome as she slid up off him and then slammed back down. Slow and deep and again and again.

He said nothing. Nor did she. But she felt the way he was forcing his breathing to stay regular. She smiled, watching him watching her breasts sway with her rhythm. She touched them, cupping them in her hands and presenting her taut nipples to his lips.

His hands lifted, tight on her thighs, and he tasted—as she wanted. She laughed, drunk on the excitement of seeing him so desperate for her.

His hands suddenly tangled in her hair, pulling her closer, his tongue rampaging into her mouth, not letting her go and giving no respite from the ferocious, powerful kisses. She half moaned, half hummed with ecstasy into his mouth as he started thrusting up to meet her—making the ride even more incredible.

The thrill rolled in on unstoppable waves, crashing over her, tossing her into a pleasure-filled place that was so captivating she alternately held her breath and then gasped for relief as they ground closer and closer again. And then she could no longer move, no longer control the ride. Her senses, her sanity crumbled under the onslaught of pure, unbearable ecstasy. His arms tightened as she quivered and then shuddered in the throes of an orgasm like no other.

As it ebbed he moved, flipping her over, crushing her beneath him. And pounded. Sliding further and harder into her heat. She clamped on him, arched up every time to pull him closer still and not let him go. With every surge of friction she was driven back to the brink. She cried out helplessly—wanting a rest but desperate for more. His breathing rasped in her ears, melding with her own broken entreaties as she chanted his name again and again. They were way past the boundaries of civility, burning now with raw, instinctive need. Blinded by sensations, beyond reason, just desperate and aching and frantic for final fulfilment.

Nothing had ever felt as amazing as him driving into her with such magnificent masculinity. Nothing could ever surpass this moment. He lifted her higher and higher with his ferocious force, filling her with power and strength and pure, sweet joy.

Her scream cracked as it became too much to bear. He reared up, grinding forward in one last, fierce long thrust, roaring his own satisfaction, tossing her body once more into convulsions of rapture and her mind into blank bliss.

Even though she could see again, she kept her eyes shut, flinging her arm over her eyes to hide awhile longer. He was close by, still half on top of her, but he'd tumbled slightly to the side so he didn't crush her. So she could breathe.

But she couldn't. Her heart galloped. She felt the vibrations of his heart thudding too, and his harsh breathing as they both fought to recover as fast as possible.

She didn't think she'd ever recover. Her whole body throbbed. Sweat slid. Her lips were so well used she was almost bruised.

An aftershock made her tremble uncontrollably. She felt his body flinch in response—and hold for a moment. But his tension didn't ease. And hers grew all the more.

Silently he took his weight on his hands and withdrew from her body.

'Excuse me a minute,' he muttered.

She didn't answer, didn't move as she listened to his footsteps recede. Then she peeped past her elbow. Empty room. Quickly she sat up and reached for her tee shirt, slipped it down as best she could. Her panties were wet and cold. Most of her was wet and cold—all heat sucked away by some giant invisible vacuum cleaner the moment he'd left the room.

Yeah, whoever it was who reckoned that sex dispelled tension was wrong. Because it was so much worse now. And not just tension—terror. What the hell had she been thinking? Rising panic sent her pulse frantic, threatening to burst her eardrums.

She struggled to her feet, stuffed her knickers into a rollerblade boot and tried to descrunch her leggings enough to be able to pull them back on. Hell, she had to get out of there as fast as possible—no way could she hold herself together if she got close to him some more. No wonder those woman wanted to warn others—he was unbelievable, and all she wanted was every bit of him, every star in the whole fantasy dream.

'Regretting it already?'

She looked up, Ethan was on the edge of the room, watching her uncoordinated movements with a towel slung round his hips and a frown on his face.

'You know *you* were the one grinding on my hand in the middle of a public park.' He stepped closer.

Her pulse went supersonic. She was shocked by his bluntness. She couldn't bear to look at his darkened eyes, or his sculpted, glistening torso, so she looked at the floor and tried to get back to decent. 'You put your hand in my pants in the first place.'

'I was merely pointing out how vulnerable you are.'

'You couldn't resist touching.'

'Because you were gagging for it.'

She stumbled as she tried to yank her leggings up, hopping on one foot with no dignity left whatsoever. She gave in. 'Yes, you live up to your reputation Ethan. You must be feeling very satisfied.'

'Absolutely not.'

Nonplussed, she shut up and sent him a wary glance. He looked grim.

'Don't you dare insinuate that I took advantage of you,' he said, his temper clearly fraying as badly as hers.

But she had to play it very cool, very sophisticated, and hide the fact her heart was still beating louder than a jackhammer and about to burst out of her mouth. 'I wasn't going to. You know I wanted it, Ethan. And I enjoyed it.' She shrugged as if it had all been nothing. 'And now I should get going.'

'Because you've had what you wanted?' he said bitterly. 'So what? You're going to go home and write about it?'

She froze, abandoning the hunt for her bra. She'd hadn't given a thought to the damn blogs and their little online war. This was nothing to do with that—this had been so much *more* to her than she'd realised even two hours ago.

The frown thundered across his brow as he obviously took her hesitation as affirmation of guilt.

'Don't write it,' he said.

Nadia turned away from him and picked up her rollerblades, knowing she'd just found the way to end it with him. To escape completely. 'But its popularity is skyrocketing.'

'It's that important to you?'

'Yes, my website is very important to me. This was just a fling.'

'You're going to detail it, then?'

'No.'

'So you're going to fabricate what you put on there?'

He thought she was going to embroider on all this? He

had to be joking. She turned back to glare at him. 'Are you setting me up?'

'So little trust, Nadia,' he said coolly. 'When you just let me right inside you.'

Yeah, that had been utter madness. 'I'm keeping on writing.'

'Then so am I.'

She swallowed. 'It'll be my perspective. Honest.' And with zero detail.

He leaned back on the arm of the chair, hands gripping the towel. 'So you're going to say you seduced me?'

'Is that what you think happened?'

'You made all the moves, honey.'

Well, not quite. But she knew what he meant. She'd given the green light. 'Only because you goaded me into it.'

'So you still don't want to take responsibility? When are you going to be honest and admit that I don't use women? That I have fun with women who are as up for it as I am. Women. Like. *You*.'

Yeah, she was one of the masses now, wasn't she? And as pulled under his spell as they'd all been. 'Not all women realise you're only up for "fun". That's why they've all flocked to warn others about you.'

'I don't cheat, Nadia. I don't ever offer them anything.'

'You do. You just don't realise it.' He offered the sun and stars and the moon and all the excitement in the universe. And then he left a big black hole.

His eyes darkened. 'So what? Unconsciously somehow I'm a jerk? Is it my fault they weave some kind of fantasy after one round of sex?'

That was a mistake she refused to make. And to avoid it she had to get out of here and away from him right now. She would not be thinking about him ever again. Not seeing him ever again. How had she ever thought she could get away with sleeping with him and come out unscathed? 'It's all about expectation. Do you make it clear from the beginning that it's only three dates?'

'I did with you.'

'You know this situation is different. This is a total fabrication. You and I would never have met ordinarily.'

He stood and the towel dropped from his hips. She closed her eyes. When she opened them again his shorts were back on and she could breathe.

'I bet you don't usually say, Hey, let's go out a couple of times, maybe fool around and then let it fizzle,' she said rawly.

'I don't know it's going to fizzle.'

'And yet it always does.' Like *hell* he was actually hunting for something more.

'I make it clear I'm not looking for anything serious.' He pulled his shirt on with vicious movements, trying to justify the unjustifiable. 'I don't like complications.'

'Why is that, exactly?'

'Because I don't like scenes like this. Why are women always so complicated?'

'All humans are complicated, Ethan. Even you.'

'I'm not. I have very simple needs.'

'All basic instinct?' she asked. 'You just haven't grown up yet. You don't want to deal with whatever it is that makes you such a commitment-phobe.' She tried to stuff her foot into a boot and realised something was in the way. She put her hand in instead and pulled out her damn knickers. She looped her hand through one leg of them and bent to pull the boot on.

He swore. 'What do you think you're doing?'

'What does it look like?'

'You're not going to skate home,' he spat. 'Absolutely not.'

'Fine.' She ditched the boot effort and stood upright again. 'I'll get a cab.'

'I'm driving you.' As barefoot as she, he snatched up his keys from the floor and stomped to the door.

Silently she followed.

He had a car as flash as his apartment and didn't need directions, so the trip was fast, the conversation nil.

'We have one more date.' Scathingly he broke the pulsing atmosphere as he pulled in front of her house. 'Friday suit you?'

Never in a million years. As far as she was concerned this whole mess was over. She was getting out of it *now*. 'I can't do Friday,' she said, just as snappily. 'I have another date.'

'Oh, you do?'

'Well, this isn't exclusive or anything, Ethan,' she lied, cauterising her heart with her burning, words. 'Do we really have to suffer through another date?'

'Oh, yeah, those screams were real *sufferance*, Nadia.'

He'd gone sceptical and she didn't blame him. But she wanted this to be over. She didn't want to have three dates and be out. It would be two and she was through. No more. Kicking him to the kerb now was the only way to ensure he'd never want to hear from her again. And then she could get over this massive, massive mistake. So, with a calculated, completely fabricated indifference, she got out of the car and walked. She clutched her blades to her chest to hold in her huge hurt heart.

'So you've had all you wanted? It was just curiosity driving you?' Ethan called after her from the open car window.

She could hear the sarcasm—and the scorn. She kept walking, hating herself more than he hated her.

'Hey, Nadia, who just used who?'

# CHAPTER EIGHT

ETHAN shoved his foot on the accelerator and the wheels screeched as he shot away from the kerb. He hated complicated, and this was beyond that. This was a mess. And why? Ordinarily he wouldn't mind at all about a date coming to its conclusion. But this hadn't been the usual flirty goodbye—this had been cold, sudden and frankly vicious.

Yes, he liked sex. He liked it and he'd had a lot of it. But he'd never had sex like that before. Not so intense and angry and hot and funny all at the same time. He'd never before been so hot he almost hadn't made it. Not so on the edge and up in the stratosphere—so good his guts were still twisted. And all he wanted right now was more. With her.

He'd not intended it to happen. Before the date this afternoon he'd been determined to play it easy—tease but don't take. That was the whole point of this damn deal anyway. Oh, of course he'd wanted to—but he'd thought he had a little more self-control. Clearly he didn't.

He got back to his flat and stalked to the shower to cool off. He was confronted by his massive bath, overflowing with bursting bubbles, and water all over the floor. Yeah—he'd turned the taps on before, gone back out to the lounge to scoop her up and put her in it with him so they could have lazy, floating, spa sex to recover. Only she'd been back in her tee and desperate to get away from him, spitting insults. Her fury completely unjustified when he had *not* scorned her. Quite the reverse.

Furiously he mopped up the mess and took a shower. Stewed over the last hour. So she'd had what she wanted and apparently she didn't want it again. Didn't want anything else. Didn't give a damn. Hell, she couldn't have spelt it out more clearly—all she'd wanted was a quick shag on the floor.

By rights that should be nothing for him to get upset about—wasn't that exactly the uncomplicated kind of hook-up he enjoyed? So why the hell was he feeling so bitter and twisted?

Because he wanted more. He wanted her again—now. But he also wanted to spar some more, and alternately laugh with it. He totally got off on the challenges she threw his way. He liked just being near her almost as much as he liked being in her. He shivered, his skin going goosefleshy despite the fact he was now standing under a jet of hot water. He crashed out of the shower, shrugged into some clothes and went to make coffee, still feeling cold despite the warmth of the late afternoon. Sick. That was the problem. Summer flu or something. That was the reason for the whole body ache.

Nadia hid in her house—blinds down like a bat avoiding the last of the sunlight. She dreaded Ethan's next blog post. How honest was he going to be? And how honest was *she* going to be? She couldn't regret having sex with him, but it had been reckless and no way could she do it again—despite the itch already spreading in her veins.

She clicked "refresh" on his blog for the forty thousandth time. It was official. She now had OCD. But still there was nothing. Blog silence. She showered and slipped into one of the "limited edition"—five hundred had been the minimum order—WomanBWarned tee shirts she'd had printed, and that were now stacked in a box tower in the corner of her room. She'd sold four. But that was a start, right?

*Ugh.* She turned her back on them and hurried back to the lounge to check his blog again. Then, when there was nothing, her e-mail. There were several posts to the forum that she should respond to. Later.

She opened a message from Megan, which included a picture of her sailing around some idyllic Greek isle with Sam.

> *OMG, we (and the rest of the planet) are so ablog over your war with the Ethan guy—too funny. You've so got to put him in his place. He sounds hot, tho— he's a possible if it weren't for the ego, right? So who cares about the ego? Just have some fun!*

Um, yeah, she'd tried that. Succeeded too—until the doubts had needled in only seconds after her multiple-orgasmic warmth had started to fade. As for putting him in his place—yeah, right. She was going to. But the wish to do that had receded—there were other things she wanted now. Like to know more about him.

She curled her feet up beneath her in her big, comfy swivel chair and stared at the font he'd chosen for his GuysGetWise banner. It, like the rest of him, told her nothing. What more did she know of him after two dates? Even now she'd had sex with him did she really know him any better? Oh, sure, she knew he was quick-witted, that he had a wickedly infectious laugh, and that when he looked at her she felt like the most captivating woman on the planet—but beyond that?

Frowning, she leaned over her keyboard. She clicked into her own blog and started typing.

*The Day Date*
*Okay, I admit it, as I did on the first date—I broke a couple of my own rules. Last time it worked against me. This time I hoped it would help me get one up on him. But it didn't—if anything it backfired completely. So take heed of those tips, girls. They're there for good reason.*

*In fairness—and I am trying to be fair here— Ethan is a nice guy. He makes an effort, he's generous and, yes, he knows how to make a woman feel good. He's courteous, he's chivalrous, he's protective. Oh, and he can talk flirt'n'dirt like no one else on earth.*

*Yet there's so much that you just don't get to know. He'll get intimate physically, if that's something you want. But emotionally?*

*That's a total no-go. I know as little of anything meaningful about him as I did before date one.*

*In my last post I questioned whether there was anything beneath that charming, handsome surface of his. But now I ask why is he so determined to hide whatever there may be?*

*Is it his way of maintaining his "mystery"? Because, if so, then hats off to him—because curiosity is a thing that will hook a woman. Yeah, his tease and trap plan works. But then he still doesn't share anything about himself, his family, what he cares about. And for most women sharing bodies isn't enough.*

*So what is it he's afraid to reveal? Maybe it's just that there really is nothing there. He's simply super-*

*ficial. So he limits the length of the game because he knows his own limitations—and that if you go for anything more than three dates, you're going to know it too.*

Ethan stared at her blog, the churning lava of his temper boiling ever closer to eruption. A reaction that he knew was more extreme than her words warranted—for had she fabricated? Had she kissed and told?

No. That was honesty he was reading, and she'd been honest and open in a surprisingly discreet way. Some hints that really only he would pick up. There was no denial of what had happened, but no blow-by-blow account either. He guessed she'd neither confirm nor deny when her blog followers asked the inevitable "did you do him?" question. Which was exactly how he'd respond when his readers asked him.

She'd done okay with her write-up. But still he hated every word. Most especially that "Ethan is a nice guy" bit. Ugh—nice. What kind of a word was *nice*? It was ironic that he'd always tried to be *nice* and now he was it seemed as flavoursome as dishwater. He didn't want to be so average, as if he was some loser she had to be kind to. He didn't need her generous, not-particularly-moved judgement, thanks.

And, while she admitted a smidgeon of responsibility, she still laid too much at *his* door. What was the crap about not knowing anything more about him? She couldn't blame that on him. Date one she'd been too busy talking about herself—which admittedly he'd engineered. Date two she hadn't asked. She'd just got out of there as fast as she could. She hadn't so much as glanced round his apartment, hadn't asked about his work or life or anything. She'd screwed, then scarpered. So how was her not getting to know him more a result of him "hiding"? What was it she wanted to know, exactly? Should he draw up a list of his favourite things? His most happy memory? It was rubbish. If she'd wanted to get to know him then she should have stuck around and spent more time with him.

He knocked back his coffee in one gulp—and got the bitter bits at the bottom. Grimacing, he stabbed the keyboard.

*Was Date Number 2 Nailed?*

With that pathetic start, he stopped. He really didn't want to answer it. Didn't know how he could without admitting what had happened—which he really didn't want to do. He didn't kiss and tell. Right to his bones he now regretted the whole online blog thing. It was such a stupid idea, and it had dumped him into something he didn't quite know how to climb out of. But he couldn't just delete the thing because he refused to let it be over with her. And the three dates deal was the one way he could catch her again. Yes, he wanted to catch her one more time. Catch her and blow her mind. So he had to respond now.

*Tease and trap—mission accomplished.*
*A surprisingly honest **OlderNWiser** even says it herself: the technique works. But she also points out the major flaw—it's only successful for a limited time.*

*Sure, I accept that. But it begs the question for how long do you want to trap? Catch and release is the aim of the game for many men. And, let's face it, lots of women love the chase and to be caught too, and are happy to go onto another game with another guy after. Therein is the excitement, the thrill. It all depends on what you're looking for, and so long as*

*you're looking for the same things then no problem,
right? It's pretty obvious with most guys.*

*Guess it's up to the ladies to be honest about what
they're looking for. In my experience they're often
not, and then the guy gets the blame for the broken
heart when in fact it was the girl who decided to play
with the matches in the first place. Think on that, all
you sweethearts out there.*

*Ms **OlderNWiser** debates my level of superficial-
ity vs. depth. I'd challenge her definition of super-
ficiality—'cos, honey, I'm not going to sit around
pontificating about politics or religion on a date.
Where's the fun in that?*

*But we have one more date to go, so let's see what
that brings. Clearly it's time to put her in touch with
my "sensitive" side. But I'm not giving away any se-
crets pre-date. We'll do it first and then I'll report
back. I can tell you it's my choice for the date, and it
is going to be nothing like what she expects.*

Ethan watched the cursor flash, unhappy with what
he'd written but unable to come up with anything better. He was still too steamed. She wanted to know more
about him? He'd let her learn a few things, for sure, and he
knew exactly how to throw her into it. He laughed at the
evilness of his idea—but she'd asked for it, after all. The
almighty great pain in the neck was that it couldn't happen for a week. He pressed "publish" then shoved away
from his desk, suddenly furious that it was so many damn
days away. Still, maybe that gave him a chance to get his
hot-for-her hormones back under control. Damn it, maybe
he'd go out on another date himself on Friday night. She'd
said this wasn't exclusive. He could go and have some real

fun with someone less trouble. He'd head to his favourite bar with the boys and see what action he could chase out.

His guts twisted painfully again, and the bitter coffee taste still burnt his tongue. Yeah, he was definitely suffering some sort of flu when the thought of hitting the scene made him feel sick.

Monday, Tuesday and Wednesday were the longest days Nadia had ever lived through. Nothing had rattled her nerves, sleep and appetite like this. Not even discovering her perfect boyfriend actually made a hobby of conning the virginity out of as many young uni students as he could—as he had her. Nope, not even that had had her as distracted or on edge as this.

She was awake more than half each night, watching the comments coming in to the blogs. It was horrific. She was so, so glad of her anonymity, and hated the fact his name was out there—even though most of the comments on his blog were bigging him up as "the man". The speculation was rife—and also right—and several comments were crass. Interestingly there hadn't been a word from the women who'd posted on the original thread. It surprised her—she'd have thought they'd be interested and amused by the challenge.

She even surreptitiously checked at work—totally fixated. She struggled to stop herself refreshing both their blogs every other minute. Most of the time she managed, but one in ten she didn't. Nothing more appeared online directly from Ethan. He didn't comment on the comments. Nor did she any more. But she was waiting. Nothing, she now knew, was as bad as waiting. He'd said they were going to do date three, yet he hadn't contacted her about it. So she was waiting, waiting, waiting. Jumping every time the phone went or her e-mail pinged, sitting on her hands to stop herself calling him. So much for never seeing him again, for getting over her fatal attraction to him. Instead she wanted to apologise for being such a cow when he'd dropped her home—wanted to suck back that bitter end to the afternoon. Only she really didn't think he'd care all that much. He just wanted to win. It was still all a game to him.

And then it happened—her mobile rang, with his number on the display. Sweat bubbled from every pore and she gulped a breath which didn't help. Her lungs and brain still shut down as excitement overrode everything. All she had in her head was the stupid hope that her voice wouldn't hit squeak territory when she said hi.

Of course it did.

Panic shot high as she waited to hear what he had to say—except she could only hear her pounding heart.

'About our next date,' he said slowly.

'You still want to do another?' she blurted.

There was a pause. Nadia closed her eyes and winced at her unintentional *entendre*. She really had to learn not to jump in on him.

'Did you think I'd let you off that easily, Nadia? A deal is a deal. Or are you backing out?'

'No. We can do the last *date*.' She spelt it out, giving him no cause to think she meant something *else*.

'I know you're already seeing someone on Friday, but can you do Saturday?'

'Yes.' She didn't correct her lie, but didn't try to play any more games by putting him off again either. This was purely about survival now. Of course if she really wanted to survive she should just say no, but she couldn't say no to him—the beating of her blood just wasn't going to let her.

'Afternoon,' he said calmly.

'Another day date?' Heat filled her face as she thought of the last one. The scent of the grass suddenly hit her, along with the remembered sensation of him pressing her into it.

'Kind of. But there won't be any exercise this time. You need to wear something a little more formal. That dress you wore to the movies would be good.'

She swallowed. No exercise, huh? His oh-so-casual attitude sharpened her antagonism. He *so* wasn't dictating her wardrobe to her. 'I can do a little more formal.'

'Great. Then I'll pick you up at one.'

'Okay. See you then.'

He rang off without saying goodbye. It made concentrating on work the rest of the day impossible. Well, not impossible, but it was extremely annoying that she had to be there and not at home so she could obsess.

She went out for a walk and bought an ice-cream—to cool herself down on the inside. Gave herself a headache by eating it too quickly. She really had to pull herself together. She was *not* going to ruin her reputation at work because of some guy she was going to see only once more. She had to get a grip. Self-pep-talked up, she went back to the office and sat down and worked overtime, losing herself in the tasks and not once going back online.

In the evening at home she texted Megan for support. He wanted a little more formal? She was going to need some help with that. Formal for day-time wasn't that easy to pull.

*Def wear dress but hair down not up. Help yourself to anything in my wardrobe.*

Saturday morning she followed Megan's advice, plaiting just a narrow section of hair near the front and then clipping it back. She totally wished she could borrow some of Meg's amazing shoes—except she'd have to stuff tissue into the toes to fit them, and that just wouldn't be a good look. She put a little more make-up on than usual—mainly to hide the signs of sleeplessness under her eyes.

Right on one o'clock she opened the door, and with a brain-draining combination of nerves, excitement and foreign shyness looked at him. Neither spoke. The moment of silence went on so long she started to panic.

'Is this not okay?' Totally husky rather squeaky this time.

'No, it's okay.' He cleared his throat at the same time she did. 'You look great.'

He was smart-casual too, and she was glad she'd gone with the little gilt heels and the silver dress. But she was melting into a puddle—awkwardness was the only thing that saved her. She wanted to apologise, she wanted to beg, she wanted to start over. She wanted so many things that were impossible.

He had his car, held the door for her to get in. She didn't look at him.

'Change the music if you want,' he said as he pulled out into the traffic.

Actually, she liked this band and their loudness. The car smelt nice—it smelt like him. 'Where are we going?'

'Oh, you know I like to preserve a little mystery,' he answered too smoothly.

She glanced at him, but he was looking hard at the road ahead and she wasn't inclined to try and start the conversation again. Nor was he—so somehow forty minutes rolled by in silent, screaming tension.

Eventually they cruised into one of those cute home counties villages—all quaint and expensive. And then he pulled into the driveway of one stunning country home. There were little pink balloons on the gate, and a line-up of flash European cars parked along the street.

Nadia's tension couldn't stay silent now. What the hell were they coming to? She slowly got out of the car and followed him to a beautiful doorway. Through the windows of the house she saw people in pretty party dress milling—and she knew.

'This is some kind of family occasion, isn't it?' Appalled, she slowly climbed the steps up to the door. All the needing-to-apologise feeling fled.

'My niece's christening, yes.'

'I can't be here.' She saw the amusement on his face and her temper flared. 'This isn't the place for you to play your manipulating games.'

'Oh? That's fine coming from you—the mistress of manipulation. Treat me mean, keep me keen—is that what you were doing?'

There was only one bit of that sentence she registered. Dumbfounded, she gazed up at him. 'You're still keen?'

'Why?' Roughly his hands snaked around her waist and he yanked her against him right there on the doorstep. 'You still want me?'

One hand slid lower, firmly curving around her butt. Through the thin shiny dress his heat burned. Her instant tremor was obvious to them both. And suddenly she felt like crying. She was tired of feeling this desperate for him. 'I wasn't playing games with you.' Oh, she sounded pathetic—and pleading.

'The hell you weren't.' His intense gaze stripped her completely.

And she was pleading now. He was vibrating too—with annoyance, and something else. Something every ounce of her wanted to believe was desire. She gazed up at him, too thrilled by the close contact to realise what she was revealing to him—too hot to care. All she wanted was this contact to become closer still.

She heard his breath catch, watched immobile as his head angled and slowly lowered, his sensual lips coming towards hers. Her own breath caught then, while her heart thundered. She tilted her chin, wanting the kiss so badly. His hands tightened, sending more pleasure shocks along her nerves. She liked feeling the strength of him.

But suddenly he looked up. Too late she registered that the door beside them had opened.

Not releasing her from his tight embrace, Ethan suddenly flashed a totally different sort of smile. 'Hello, Mother.'

# CHAPTER NINE

'ETHAN! It's you.' The woman sounded stunned. 'You and...'

Nadia flinched, felt his muscles spasm too. Suddenly it registered that she was resting all her weight against him. But she couldn't pull away. The steel band across her back—i.e. his arm—wouldn't let her. Desperately she licked her lips, so she could manage a smile, and turned her head to face the one woman she'd never, ever expected to meet.

'Ethan?' Another voice, and then two other, younger women materialised to flank his mother's sides.

'Mother, meet Nadia. Nadia, this is my mother, Victoria, and my two sisters Jessica and Polly.' The mocking amusement in his voice was apparent, but it didn't chase the surprise off all their faces.

Nadia wished he'd let her go so she could run away to a small dank cave. But he still held her far, far too closely. She shook her head slightly to dispel her fuzzed vision—only the situation dived drastically when she saw his family clearly. Ethan the Gorgeous just *would* have two glamorous, swan-like sisters and a model-of-class-and-refinement kind of mother.

'How lovely to meet you.' Polly swapped a look with

her sister. 'See—this is why I had to pick up Mother, instead of Ethan.'

'Well, it wasn't like *you* were going to bring a date.' Ethan said, still not releasing Nadia from the inappropriate clinch.

'We didn't expect you to either,' Polly snapped back. It took five crucifying silent seconds for her to realise the her gaffe before she blustered with a sheepish smile, 'Of course it's wonderful you could be here, Nadia. You have *no idea* how thrilled were are to meet you.'

Nadia kept digging her fingers into his shirt, trying to push him away, but the man-mountain wasn't moving. She could feel the slow, deep rise and fall of his chest against her cheek—completely tantalising and scattering her focus. 'Oh, thank you so much,' she babbled to cover her confusion and embarrassment. 'I'm so sorry to be here unexpectedly. I hope it's no trouble. I really don't want to intrude…' She stumbled over the words and felt her flush deepening. 'I can—'

'Come right in.' Ethan suddenly moved, turning and pushing her slightly ahead of him with firm hands on her upper arms.

The three women stepped back into the house. Nadia walked past them and kept walking to the nearest corner—quite a distance in the stunning large atrium she found herself in. Ethan kept pace.

'I'm not staying here,' she hissed, facing him.

'You have to now.' He grinned down at her, looking too relaxed all of a sudden. 'This way you can get to know more about me—my family and my history and all those fascinating, irrelevant things women want to know. I'm sure my sisters would love to fill you in on a few facts.'

Oh, so *this* was his way of showing her more about himself? She shook her head—he was unbelievable, and now she was stuck here, with no wheels to get away. Of course her curiosity was ravenous…and he knew it.

From the stunned look on his mother's and his sisters' faces she figured him bringing a date wasn't an everyday occurrence. But she knew not to read any significance into it—this was all about their little war.

'This is so impolite,' she told him, hoping for a last minute escape.

'There was me thinking you were an expert at being impolite.'

She swallowed that, then fired right back. 'You were the one keeping us in that shocking clinch on the step.'

His grin broadened back to wicked. 'It would have been much more of a shock if I'd let you go and they'd seen how hard I was.'

Nadia flushed, both mortified and melting again. 'You really think it's okay for me to be here?' She gazed up at his laughing façade and saw the shadows lurking in the back of them.

'As long as you don't get too close to me again while there are people around,' he murmured.

'There's a little service at the church down the road in a few minutes, and then it's back here for afternoon tea on the lawn.' Polly crossed the atrium and interrupted them.

'Oh.' Nadia smiled through her breathlessness. 'Is there anything I can do to help?'

Ethan laughed. 'Jess and Polly have this thing planned with military precision. You can just be decorative, like me. Is *he* here?' That last to his sister.

Polly nodded with a helpless sort of shrug. 'But alone.'

Nadia didn't miss the look that flashed between the two of them. Who were they talking about?

'Hey, I haven't had a chance to say congratulations on

the latest league tables,' Polly added suddenly. 'Most bill-able hours, biggest revenue earner in the year to date. Way to—'

'Don't try to impress her, Polly,' Ethan interrupted drily. 'She sees through to my "internetorious" nature.'

Polly's eyes widened and she looked flustered. 'I wasn't thinking of Nadia. I was thinking you should tell *him*.'

Ethan just grunted.

Polly sighed and turned the sheepish smile on Nadia again. 'Come on, we'd better get going.'

The church was only a few minutes away, and all the guests walked in a festive procession. Nadia walked near the front, with Ethan still keeping a courteous hand at her back. She wished he wouldn't. It made her skin there sing—while the rest of her yearned for more of his touch. Deep in her belly the urge for payback burned, but increasingly she doubted she had the skill to play these games with Ethan. She didn't really know the rules.

To keep herself on track she focused on watching the little girl at the very front, the one all dressed up in a pretty pink confection and bouncing around as if she was on a sugar high.

'That's Isabella, Jess's eldest.' So Ethan was watching her too.

It seemed everyone else was watching *them*. As they stood circling the font during the service, she caught several people looking at her and at Ethan, and at the way he now held her hand tightly—not from affection, but so she couldn't inch away from where he stood too close. Near the back of the group there was a gaggle of beautiful women in beautiful dresses, and they all had hungry features when they looked at Ethan. Even those women obviously in a couple glanced at them too often, curiosity bright in their eyes. Nadia felt more midget-like than ever, and dreaded the tea party to follow. She suspected she was in for some unsubtle grilling. And she was right.

'Meet Nadia.'

Over and over again he introduced her, never once applying any description to her name—no *my date*, Nadia, no *my friend*, Nadia, no *bitch queen*, Nadia—and of course no one there was impolite enough to ask. Yes, he was a master at preserving the mystery. She met uncles, aunts, cousins, family friends, an endless stream of people involved in Ethan's life. And she was too acutely aware of his presence at her side to be able to learn anything much.

'I'll get you another drink,' he murmured, relieving her of her empty champagne glass. 'We'll switch to lemonade now, huh? Wouldn't want you getting too hot from the wine.'

She ignored the wicked look he threw her, too nervous about being left alone to face questions to be able to rise to the banter. She turned towards the garden, hoping to avoid everyone, and followed a path between billowing roses, reaching out to touch some of the soft, perfect petals.

'Beautiful, aren't they?'

Nadia glanced up. From the other side of a crimson rose-laden bush, an older man held out a glass of champagne to her. To her surprise she recognised the smooth voice—but not his face. She took the glass he offered with a slight smile and rummaged round her useless mind. 'Yes, they are.'

'I like that one best—*Grüss an Tepliz*.' He pointed to the red ones and added with a smile. 'My name's Matthew.'

Of course, she had it now—Matthew Rush. He was a veteran political correspondent. She'd heard him do hundreds of interviews on the radio in the morning, when her parents had been listening as they'd got ready for work. She'd been "shushed" so many times for talking during this guy's reports. Matthew *Rush*—so in what way was he related to Ethan?

'I'm Nadia.' She smiled and took the tiniest sip from her glass. Ethan had actually been right in knowing she didn't want more, but she wanted to be polite. 'I like these.'

Matthew nodded. 'Good choice. *Souvenir de la Malmaison.* Polly planted them for Jess a couple of years ago. She did a great job.'

'Yes, they're amazing.' Nadia walked further into the display.

'This one has an incredible scent.' Matthew touched a bush smothered in milky blooms. *'Madame Alfred Carrière.'*

'Nadia.'

Nadia turned at the sharp interruption. Ethan stood at the beginning of the grassy path. She could feel the waves of hostility from here. She snatched a quick glance at the man by her side. But Matthew Rush wasn't giving anything away.

'Ethan,' he said calmly.

'Dad.' Ethan clipped the iciest answer back.

Nadia couldn't have broken the huge, gaping silence even if she tried. Matthew Rush was Ethan's *dad*?

Finally Ethan turned to her and spoke, his voice betraying a roughness that his father's polished-for-radio tones never would. 'I'll show you the boathouse. Jess has just had it redecorated.'

'Okay—great.' She nodded and walked, sending Matthew a smile for farewell, completely confused as to why Ethan had suddenly turned into the ice man.

'I didn't know Matthew Rush is your father,' she said, just for something to say.

He didn't answer—just kept walking until they were both out of earshot and view of the other guests, until they were in front of the cute restored wooden boathouse. Only then did he turn and face her.

Nadia swallowed when she saw his expression—tight, pale, too controlled. He was angry. Angrier than the day he'd stormed in to see her at work and threatened to sue her. So angry she felt adrenalin surge into every cell, preparing her to *fight*. Except she didn't know about what.

'He's pretty famous,' she added, still confused. 'I've heard so many of his reports.' He'd written a book too, if she remembered right. And now the interviewer himself got interviewed.

'Yeah, you and he would hit it off. You have a lot in common. The need to make yourself important. To be heard by a lot of people. To be recognised.' Ethan almost snarled.

Okay, she knew she was missing something major, but he didn't need to go off at her. 'There's a flaw in your analysis, Ethan.' She wasn't going to let him get away with insults just because he'd been hit by a freak bad mood. 'Your father seeks fame under his own name. I'm anonymous. WomanBWarned isn't about me—it's about making a difference. I'm not taking advantage of my relationships to make a name for myself. In fact *you're* the one who put our dates out there for everyone to read.'

He glared at her. She watched closely for the steam to start shooting from his ears.

'Maybe *you're* like your father,' she said blandly. 'Wanting to be popular.'

Colour flooded into his cheeks. 'I'm nothing like him.'

'Really?' His vehemence intrigued her. 'Why? What's he like?'

'Isn't it obvious?' he snapped. 'Hell, how do you think it makes me feel to see him hitting on the girl I brought here?'

'*What?*' Nadia gaped. Then giggled. A lot. 'Ethan, he wasn't hitting on me. We were talking about the roses.'

But Ethan wasn't seeing the funny side. Ethan was glowering all the more. 'I've known the guy a whole lot longer than you. I've seen that look before.'

She shook her head—the idea was outlandish. 'You've had too much champagne in the sun. You're seeing things.' But her humour died when he still didn't lighten up. He really thought his own father had been flirting with her? That she'd go along with that? 'You know, it's completely insulting of you to think that I'd—'

'I know *you* wouldn't,' he snapped. 'But he would.'

Nadia thought about it. She hadn't seen Matthew up at the front near Ethan's mum during the christening. She hadn't seen Ethan talk to him. There'd been some veiled comment from Polly when they'd arrived—about who'd been going to bring their mum, about whether "he" was here. And "him" being here alone had been major enough for Polly to point it out. She didn't need a psychology degree to figure his parents had split—and that it wasn't amicable. And that there'd probably been adultery issues. Yeah, now she thought about it, some *would* think Matthew was suave. She'd just thought he was old.

She nibbled the inside of her lip and tried not to stare at how uncomfortable Ethan looked. Fiercely defensive, but vulnerable, he turned away from her. She melted, and the desire to reassure him rose—she wished she understood what scar it was that had just been ripped open. 'Ethan, your father was nothing but charming to me.'

'Yeah, he's always charming to women.'

Nadia half smiled and answered softly, 'So are you.'

Sharply he faced her, but said nothing. Slowly the blaze in his eyes died out, leaving a hint of something like hurt. And he just looked at her. And the longer he looked, the more that hint of hurt seemed to grow. She didn't understand why.

His lips parted, she heard the indrawn breath, and she waited, her own breath bated.

Piercing shrieks made them jump three feet apart.

'Ethan, can you help me?' Jessica hurried towards them, struggling to carry a very red-faced, wriggling toddler. 'Bella's having a meltdown, I need to feed the baby and Tom needs to entertain the guests—and Polly's working hard to keep Mother away from Father.'

'Sure—give her to me.' All calm, Ethan reached out for the wailing child.

'I'm so sorry to interrupt.' Jess looked apologetically at Nadia. 'What must you think of us?'

Nadia didn't know what to think.

'She's just feeling out of sorts.' Jess looked panicky as Bella geared up for another bellow.

'She's not the only one,' Ethan muttered, getting his niece out of his sister's earshot. 'How good are you at entertaining little kids?' He looked desperately at Nadia.

'Hopeless,' she whispered, but she followed. They bypassed the guests and circled wide back to the house. By the time they got inside the girl's wails had lessened as her Uncle Ethan spoke quietly to her.

Nadia opened the door that Ethan pointed to, stepped in after him, and then closed it again. A music room. And Ethan was at the baby grand piano.

'You have to stop crying because you have to help me play,' he told the child. 'You know I can't play without your help.'

Bella sat on his knee, he put his hands on the keys, and she put her hands on top of his. It was obviously a game that had been played many times before. She was smiling now. So was Ethan. He started, got four bars into a really stodgy sort of grade three piece. Nadia bit her lips to stop laughing—it was sweet, really—and suddenly realised she was falling deeper into complete 'like' with a guy she'd been so sure was a shark.

But then Bella interrupted. 'No, no. Not that one. The other one.'

'You're sure about that?'

Nadia recognised the teasing tone in Ethan's words. She saw Bella did too. So this was part of a shared joke—a routine that had to be adhered to.

He started to play again, and Nadia was stunned into immobility. Despite the burden of a little person on his knee he played magnificently. Notes thundered as his fingers crashed over the keys. Bella glowed with excitement as her hands rode fast on his. A massive, loud passionate piece from Rachmaninov, huge and echoing and—hell, she'd had no idea Ethan could play so well.

'Play it again?' Bella asked, even though the last note hadn't stopped vibrating round the room.

Ethan groaned and turned to spot Nadia. 'Come and sit beside us. We can't play again unless you do.'

Reading the look on the girl's face, Nadia moved quickly.

Ethan laughed as she did and shuffled along the seat to make room. 'Do you play?'

'Not that good stuff. I was stuck with Mozart. My hands are too small to cope with any of the great romantics.'

'Not so bad to be stuck with Mozart.' He cuddled the little girl closer. 'Play some now.'

His mood had been restored even more than the child's. He was back to smiling and charming and gorgeous, and Nadia was floored. 'I'm not as good as you, and I haven't played in a really long time.'

'I disagree with the former but am well aware of the latter.'

She looked balefully at him. 'Do you think along those lines all the time?'

'Around you? Absolutely.'

'Play, play, play,' Bella interrupted petulantly, completely missing the undertones.

'Yeah, Nadia,' Ethan said slyly. 'Play.'

She sighed, hiding her smile, and put her hands in position. It really had been a while. But years and years of practice couldn't be completely forgotten. After a few bars she began to enjoy it, giggling when she stumbled over the odd passage, but soon getting the feel for it again, losing track of time as she worked through her favourite piece. A quiet one—not the kind of rollercoaster ride of emotion up and down the stave that Ethan had crashed through.

'Keep playing,' he whispered in her ear.

She glanced sideways and saw Bella was fast asleep in his arms. Amusement warmed her. Oh, to be a kid again and fall asleep at the flick of a switch. He carefully edged off the stool. Nadia did as he'd asked and kept playing the soft sonata, turning her head a couple of times to see Ethan carefully putting his niece on the sofa near the big fireplace. He glanced at her and mouthed 'keep playing' again.

She nodded, glad to turn back so she wouldn't have to go like goo inside, seeing him be so tender. She started the piece for a third time, even more gently, waiting for the word that it was okay to stop.

There wasn't a word. There was touch. Hands—large hands—cupped her shoulders and then slid down the length of her arms to her hands. She bent her head and stopped playing.

'I think you play beautifully,' he whispered softly, his cheek brushing against hers.

She only had to turn a fraction to kiss him.

'We'd better get back out there,' he said, as if it was the last thing he wanted to do.

'Of course.' It was the last thing she wanted to do too.

They tiptoed out of the room, closing the door on the calm inside. She paused, not wanting to go back to the lawn. He stood still too, looking at her.

'Nadia…'

She knew he wanted to kiss her. And she wanted to kiss him. No games this time—just because it would feel so good. So right. But something was stopping him, and Nadia didn't know what.

'Where is she?' Jess appeared in the hall.

Ethan turned away and answered. The relief on Jess's face revealed the stress she'd been feeling. Ethan put his arm along his sister's shoulder and teased, 'Soothing irritable girls is my speciality.'

Nadia didn't know if that was a coded message to her or not. But the fact was she didn't want to be soothed. She wanted to be stirred.

Ethan chatted to his sister for a few minutes more, but the second Jess wandered away to mingle, Ethan's teasing façade dropped and he looked plain tired. No wonder. She'd just seen how hard he worked to be the charming guy who held it together for the women in his family even when he was at the very end of his own patience. But he'd masked it, protectively cared for Bella—and Jess—a gently wicked joker who'd made them feel better. But right now he looked like the one who needed help to feel better. She wished he'd talk to her. But why would he open up to his opponent in this stupid fight of theirs? She knew he was mortified by his mistake about his father, and she didn't want to embarrass him more, but there was something there and she wanted to know.

'I'd never have thought you'd play the piano like that,' she said to lighten the atmosphere. 'You look too rugby.'

He managed a grin. 'The girls had to learn. I got sent along too. They never liked it enough to practise.'

'But you did?'

He nodded briefly. 'Let's get out of here.'

People were departing, so it wasn't as if they were the first to leave, but Nadia was glad they weren't going to be the last.

'You outdid yourself, Jess. Again.' Ethan gave his sister another hug.

'Thank you very much,' Nadia said to Jess. 'It was the most beautiful afternoon tea I've ever seen. Everything was so perfect.' She wasn't lying. The décor, the food, the style of it all had been amazing.

Jess smiled at her. So did Polly.

'It would be really nice to see you again some time, Nadia,' Polly called after them.

With an uncomfortable ache in her heart Nadia kept walking to his car and pretended she hadn't heard. She couldn't face another forty minutes of silence on the drive back so she went for light, safe conversation.

'So tell me about your work. All those billable hours, huh? Are you prosecution or defence?'

Ethan gripped the steering wheel even tighter. Oh, hell, he really hadn't told her anything—and he grimaced about telling her now. He didn't do the save-the-innocent barrister act, and if she really was all about 'making a difference' then she was going to be disappointed. Still, he was used to that—right? His dad had never got over his decision to go corporate rather than chasing after the Queen's Counsel dream, despite the fact Ethan earned more now than he'd ever have done in chambers. But for his father it was all about public prestige. For Nadia it was that higher purpose thing—which meant she was going to be even more sceptical than his dad.

'I'm not a barrister,' he said heavily. 'I don't go to court and present arguments to a judge.'

'Oh? What do you do, then?'

'Corporate.' His discomfort was stupid, because his job was unbelievably competitive. 'I'm an aviation specialist.'

She frowned. 'Aviation?'

Yeah, there wasn't that much adulation in that. 'As in big deals between big airlines and aircraft manufacturers. Leasing and financing and stuff.'

'And that's law?'

'They need legal advice to do the deals—so, yes.'

'Oh.'

'It's very interesting.' Hell, did he sound desperate for approval or what? But he loved it. Wouldn't work crazy hours if he didn't.

'I'm sure.'

'It's more interesting than HR.' Totally defensive now.

'Well, that wouldn't be hard.' She laughed suddenly. 'So, does that mean you get to go for rides in flash private planes?'

'The question everyone asks.' He rolled his eyes. 'I expected more from you. Sometimes—not often.'

'But you like planes?'

'Always have. I like flying.'

'*Can* you?'

'I have my pilot's licence.' And he sky-dived. He liked the rush of that.

'Oh, that's cool. So you really love it?'

'Yeah, I do.' Finally the grin broke out of him. 'Going to work is fun. But it's not what people think of when you tell them you're a lawyer.'

'Who cares?' she said. 'You work in a field you love. You're lucky. Your parents must be proud.'

Ethan sent her a sideways look, but she was smiling ahead at the road, all innocence. Yeah, right. She was fishing, but he wasn't biting. Because, no, his father *wasn't* proud. 'You mean you don't love HR? But you get to make people miserable, right?' He teased his way out of answering.

'Very funny.'

'So why did you get into it if it's not floating your boat?'

'I wanted a job in a big firm. All big firms need HR people.'

'Why big?'

'The usual reasons—money, security.'

'Yeah, but bigger isn't always better.'

'You're wrong.' She shook her head. 'It was nice meeting your family.'

*Nice*—great. That awful word again. And she couldn't possibly think it had been nice. She was back to fishing. Apprehension slithered down his spine. Inviting her into his life this way had been crazy. How was she going to report back to her web-witches? He figured he'd be in for a caning. But had she seen his family's vulnerability? Did she even care? What about Bella? Those moments by the piano that had filled him with pleasure before now made him wince. Did Nadia think he was superficial enough to have orchestrated that? She was so untrusting she probably did. He wanted to skip this as the third date. They should do something else. But that would mean seeing her again— and that seemed like a really dumb idea. This wasn't the game it had been, and it sure as hell wasn't uncomplicated.

As he pulled up outside her flat he knew he had to address it. 'Please don't write about today in your blog.' Annoyed at how husky he sounded, he spoke faster, more harshly. 'I don't want all that out there. Not Dad. And I didn't set that up with Bella to prove anything to you. Can't—?'

'Do you think I don't know that?' she interrupted, her voice shrill. 'Do you really think I'd mention any of that?'

He was silent.

In the confines of his car her anger reverberated. Her outrage. Her hurt.

'What kind of a person do you think I am?' she asked, totally wounded. 'You haven't gotten to know *me* at all, have you? You haven't listened to anything I've told you.' She leapt out of the car and ran up her path.

Ethan stared after her—hating himself even more than he had that moment almost two hours ago. He'd felt sick when he'd seen his father talking to Nadia. He'd seen the look. It was how *he* looked at her—as if she was some delicate morsel to be devoured. Nadia had been wrong. Or maybe she'd been right and it was just that Ethan was so paranoid about his father he couldn't see straight.

Either way it didn't matter, because the revelation was still clear and still true. He'd always said he was nothing like his father, but Nadia had said differently. And he *was* the same—every bit the same selfish, insensitive jerk. He'd just proved it.

He swore and leaped out of the car.

'Nadia!' He grabbed the front door handle so she couldn't open it and get away from him. But she didn't turn around. A slender, silver fairy-woman stood in front of him—one he wanted to pull back against him and keep her there. He ached for the hot, sweet relief to be found with her.

He bent his head, lightly brushing his lips in her hair, hoping she couldn't feel it as he breathed in her scent. 'I'm sorry.'

'It doesn't matter.'

'It does.' He felt her trembling.

'I don't blame you for thinking I'd do that,' she said softly.

But he should have known she wouldn't. Deep down he had. Nadia, with her big green eyes and her sweetheart-shaped face, wasn't in this world to hurt people. Now Nadia herself was hurt—and it was his fault.

'I wish you'd talk to me,' she whispered.

'And tell you what?' His blood chilled. There wasn't anything to say. 'Don't think you know anything more about me just because you've met my messed-up family.'

'But wasn't that the point?'

He clenched his teeth. The original point had been to make her uncomfortable. Only it had backfired completely, and he was the one feeling tortured and embarrassed and angry.

'How you act around them tells me a lot.' Her voice wobbled.

He shook his head. 'It doesn't.' She knew nothing—because he'd only realised a couple of things himself this very moment. He gripped the door handle even harder, physically fighting the urge to take her into his arms.

'You're not the carefree guy you make yourself out to be. You're more sensitive than that. You care about them.'

It was so ironic that now she thought she was seeing some good in him, when he was realising just how little there actually was. 'You don't know anything, Nadia.'

She'd been right. He did hide what was beneath his surface—because underneath lurked the same kind of indifference that his father had. Indifference to relationships, commitment, marriage. Sure, he had passion for his career, but none for the burden of family and responsibility—and certainly not a woman's happiness. So he wasn't going to get into a relationship and hurt someone over and over, like his father had his mother. And Nadia was a relationship girl through and through—romantic, idealistic, a little bruised and misguided, but soft-hearted still for all that. And, for whatever warped reason, those qualities were endearing her all the more to him. But it was dangerous for her, because he would never be the right guy. Which meant he had to walk *now*.

He breathed deep to try and push out the pain cutting into his heart, but it was a mistake. Her scent curled tighter around him. Her proximity was tantalising—her soft, warm limbs and passion were so close. She didn't move. Her head was bent as she waited in silence—for what? The inevitable? He had to rebel against that.

He released the handle and pushed the door so it swung open. She stepped inside. Not following her was the hardest thing he'd ever done in his life.

It was so unfair that doing something right felt so wrong.

# CHAPTER TEN

NADIA stared at the blank form on her screen. For a long time. Then she clicked in the corner to close it. Three days later and she still hadn't posted anything online. That was for ever. Her hit rate would start to slide. Already people were commenting and asking questions. Questions she didn't want to answer.

Her mobile rang. She picked it up and checked the screen; the number was withheld which meant it wasn't him. Her heart accelerated anyway. 'Hello?'

'You haven't updated your blog.'

Okay—it was him. 'Neither have you.' She managed a light answer. There'd been no posts—no comments, e-mails, texts or phone calls either in the last three days. That was for ever and *ever*. The only thing stopping her from going insane was the thought that he hadn't sent her the flick-off flowers yet, like the women on the original *3 Dates and You're Out* thread said he did. Then again, he probably didn't feel the need to keep her sweet. They'd done the three dates. It was all over and out.

'A gentleman always lets the lady go first.'

'I'm not ready to write it yet.' Nadia turned away from her screen, screwed her eyes shut as she boldly went down the road she'd been fantasising about for the last three eternally long days and nights. 'There's a problem.'

'What kind of problem?'

She pressed her hand on her chest to stop her heart beating out of it, and blurted the words she'd rehearsed too many times to be natural. 'I can't say those claims are wrong when one major aspect is completely right.'

'What aspect's that?'

'That it's three dates and you're out. You're totally doing that to me.'

She heard the whistle of indrawn breath from his end of the phone. 'You want a fourth? You want us to go out again?'

Oh, she wanted way more than that. But right now she'd take what she could get. 'I just can't see how I can refute what those women say when we've only gone for three.'

'But you're planning to refute some other things?'

He didn't sound as pleased about that as she'd thought he would. Truthfully, she didn't want to write another word on it.

'Nadia, you know what'll happen if we meet up again.'

She waited, nibbling her lip so hard it hurt.

He cleared his throat. 'Is that something you're willing to risk?'

'Life's no fun without a little risk.' She bit harder, waiting for his reply, her nerves teetering on a cliff-edge.

'Well, there's risky and there's reckless. I told myself not to see you again.'

'Well, you don't have to.' She held her breath, held back the hurt. And waited.

For ever.

'But I think I do,' he said on a groan. 'Let's go out for dinner. We've not done the traditional date, have we? Only I'm out of town for a few days. Can you do Friday?'

'Sure.' Friday was months away. 'Where are you?'

'In Germany, trying not to think about you.'

'Are you succeeding?'

'Well, I'm calling you now, so I guess not.'

Her whole body curled into a smile. Noise broke up the line—talking in the background got louder.

'I have to go.' His voice came and went. 'You'd better put something on the blog. You'll lose people.'

'So had you.'

'I don't have time. I'll see you Friday.'

Nadia hung up and turned to her computer, determined to get some work done now.

The next morning she went back onto his blog to see if he'd put anything up. Nothing. But she noticed some of the worst comments had been taken down, and there was a note from Ethan to say that he'd be approving the comments before they got posted from now on. It seemed he'd suffered an attack of gallantry. Or was it just that he was worried about what his work colleagues would say? No, she guessed he didn't really give a damn about what other people thought of him, considering what he'd put out there. Which made her wonder more about why he'd hunted her down as the creator of WomanBWarned—what was it that had bothered him so much?

Underneath that arrogant playboy attitude Ethan really was a nice guy. He liked women, and he treated them well when he was with them. He just didn't want true intimacy or a relationship. The smoking remains of his parents' relationship had to be the cause of his reluctance. Whatever had happened had put him off committing, and he and his father were clearly at war. Which meant all she'd ever be was another one of those women he'd had a fling with. Except she had just got to date four—the final frontier. And, yes, deep inside that very stupid part of her wanted so much more. He was so easy to fall for.

The days didn't pass fast enough. She went shopping.

She went for a manicure. She went indoor speed-skating to burn energy and make her tired enough to sleep. It didn't work. So by the time Friday night rolled around she was ready too early and beside herself with anticipation. She practised yogic breathing and waited. Waited some more. Tried not to look at her watch every ten seconds. Only made it to fifteen once and got so mad with herself she took her watch off. She had her fab new dress, matching fingernails and toenails—the bits in between buffed and polished too.

But time ticked on and on and there was no knock at the door. The summer sun set and Nadia sat frozen in her chair.

Finally her phone beeped. A text message. She knew what it was before she even looked at it. He didn't even have the decency to talk to her. Tears tumbled and she was so glad Megan was still away and not there to see her humiliation. She couldn't bear to admit what a fool she was. According to the text he'd been delayed at work and missed his flight. He was on a later one and wouldn't get in until it was too late for dinner.

She totally didn't believe him. He just didn't want to do dinner at all. He never had. She'd just pushed him into something he didn't want to do and he was trying to get out of it lightly—like always.

Ethan had been trying to forget her. They'd done the three dates, so he could think about something else for five minutes now. He could find some other woman attractive. He could do nothing but work for fifty-six hours straight.

He'd only managed the last one.

He checked his phone again. Still no reply. He didn't want to call and speak to her because she wasn't going to be in a mood to listen to him. He hated letting her down. He hated how complicated this had become—but he *had* to see her again. His body wasn't letting him do otherwise, nor would his brain. She was all he could think about. All he wanted. So he'd make his apology in person. He'd make it up to her in person. But that wasn't going to help in the next few hours. He quickly punched in another number.

'Polly, I need a favour. Big favour. You've got to take your best ever bunch of flowers to Nadia.'

'Oh, Ethan,' she wailed at him. 'We liked her.'

Ethan gritted his teeth. 'So do I. So send the damn things, will you? And say I'm sorry on the card.'

'Sorry for what?'

'None of your business. But get them to her now.'

'So it isn't over?'

'It will be if you don't get them organised.'

'Okay.'

The doorbell rang. Nadia saw herself in the hall mirror as she went to answer it and swore at her panda eyes. Still, at this time of night it could only be a telecoms salesperson or something—so what did it matter.

It was a courier. He handed her the biggest bunch of flowers she'd ever seen.

Nadia took them without a word and slammed the door. The card was typed in an old-fashioned typewriter font.

*I'm sorry.*

She tossed the flowers on the table and tore the note in two, then three, and chucked the bits like pity party confetti.

How had he managed to get them out at this hour? Florists didn't work this late. He must have planned the whole thing hours ago. *Days* ago. In fact she now figured he'd totally set her up. She'd been the one to suggest another date. He'd got her in the palm of his hand just as he'd wanted and now he'd crushed her.

Her eyes were drawn back to the bright mass of blooms. Yes, they were beautiful, but she hated them. The flick-off flowers. Just as the women on WomanBWarned had said. She wiped away more scalding tears and sniffed. Why had she been so stupid as to expect anything else?

There she'd been, actually feeling something like sorry for him—trying to figure out why he avoided everything: emotional intimacy, relationships, conflict. Thinking she understood more after seeing his family the other day. But he'd so taken her for the fool she was. He was an all out jerk with not a shred of sensitivity. And right now he was laughing at her something awful.

Furious, she had to do something—anything—to feel better. And that didn't include talking to honeymoon-happy Megan. She didn't want anyone she knew to know what an idiot she'd been. But she had to vent to someone. She went into her WomanBWarned admin database and hunted. Ten minutes later she'd fired off e-mails to the other women who'd posted on the original thread. She wasn't going to put this up on the internet, but she was *so* having a private rant with them. She'd bond with others who bore the wounds—the humiliation—of being an Ethan Rush conquest. She'd snarl and moan and gnash her teeth, but not with anyone she knew.

First she just asked if they were who she thought they were, and what other info they wanted to share.

She glared at the flowers, tempted to put them in the rubbish, but she put them in Megan's room instead. Marching back, she clicked 'send/receive' ten times on her e-mail but nothing landed. She stalked to the bathroom and ran a super-hot shower, getting rid of the hair product and the panda eyes and the floral scent of her favourite perfume. She yanked on one of her WomanBWarned tee shirts and some boxers. Not that she was going to bed—sleep was impossible now. Instead she did a final check on the forums and stepped away from the computer. She'd hear the ping of e-mails from the computer if those sisters replied. There was only one thing left to do. Drink wine and watch movies. Horrors—a corpse-fest, with scary music and evil, evil monsters. She'd work her way through the all the *Nightmares on Elm Street*. To put things into perspective.

She'd watched a ton of gory numbers with her brother and initially she'd been stoic through them so as not to be the 'scared little girl' he'd expected. Now she just plain liked them. Things could be so much scarier and worse than real life. And she'd eat eye-watering chilli with it— to terrify her tastebuds too. Provide an extreme sensory experience to overwhelm the extreme agony inside.

She was twenty minutes into the third instalment when her doorbell buzzed again. Way too late for a salesman this time. Or anyone. Nerves fluttered and she paused the movie, telling herself not be scared by something Hollywood had invented. Just because it was almost two in the morning it didn't mean there was going to be a disfigured guy with knives for fingers on the other side of the door.

She opened it a fraction, and then let it swing wide.

'What are you doing here?' The strangest cocktail of feelings flooded through her—a heady mix of disbelief, relief, pleasure and uncertainty.

'I just got into Gatwick.'

'You really were stuck on a plane?'

'You didn't believe me?' His bag thudded at his feet. 'I knew you wouldn't. That's why I got Polly to send the flowers. But you still didn't reply.'

'I figured if you were in a plane you wouldn't get a text anyway.'

'No, you just don't believe me. Or trust me. Or—'

'Or what?' Her defensiveness reared. 'You sent me "see ya later" flowers.'

He frowned. 'The note was supposed to say I'm sorry.'

'It did.'

He closed his eyes and breathed deep. 'Okay, I shouldn't have come here now. It's late and we're both grumpy.' He picked up his bag.

'No.' Recovering from the shock, she grabbed his arm. 'You look shattered. Come in and have a coffee or something.'

She'd so go for the 'or something', but he really did look shattered—unshaven, red-rimmed eyes, crumpled clothes, pale.

He didn't move, even though she was using most of her weight to tug his arm. 'You didn't make other plans when I cancelled?'

'Sure I did.' She tugged harder. 'I've got movies loaded and a huge amount of ice-cream.'

He stepped in, the thinnest gleam piercing the dullness of his eyes. 'So there isn't anyone else on your sofa?'

'Is that what you were worried about?' She dropped his arm. 'That's what you're checking up on?'

'You told me this wasn't exclusive.'

'What did you expect me to say?' She shut the door behind him. 'I have some pride, you know.'

'I'm well aware of that.' He finally cracked a grin. 'So what's the movie?'

'A horror.'

'I hate horrors. They make me feel sick.'

'I'll hold your hand in the scary bits, if you like.'

Ethan managed another smile, but he was seriously out

on his feet. He shouldn't have come, but somehow when he'd got into the cab at the airport, hers had been the address he'd given. Now he was here the tiredness had hit him—right when he didn't want it to. But, oddly, it was relief wiping out the last scrap of energy—relief at seeing her wide green eyes fill with the sparkle of promise, pleasure, desire.

Her sofa was fantastically big and he sank into it. He wanted her, but he couldn't even move. Could hardly keep his eyes open. Everything overwhelmed him.

'I didn't sleep,' he mumbled.

'You spent the whole time awake?'

'Lots of work.' And that was true. They'd worked crazy long hours to close the deal. And in the few short hours he'd had to catch some ZZZs, all he'd done was toss and turn and think about Nadia. The more he tried not to, the more he had. In the end he'd decided to see her again and get her out of his system. Somehow.

'You mean you were in German lap-dancing bars twenty-four-seven.'

He laughed. It turned into a groan because the energy required was too much. 'I'm sorry. I'm rubbish company. I'm too tired.' He should go home. He didn't want to. Nor did he want to let her down any more—and he was already.

'Shut up,' she said, sounding bored. 'I'm watching the movie.'

As if to prove it, she turned the volume up a notch.

Even though his eyes were closed he grinned, loving the way she was being so nice to him—in her fashion. He just needed a short snooze and then he'd be all over her. Oh, he so would.

'Ethan?'

Nadia stared down at him in amazement. He'd hooked his legs up on the sofa, his feet dangling off the end, and he'd lain down, using her lap as his pillow. Which was nice. And frustrating. Because now he didn't answer. How could anyone fall asleep during a horror film? In less than three minutes?

She lifted her hand and tentatively stroked his jaw with the tips of her fingers, enjoying the rough stubble. Ethan Rush was an exhausted man. She sat back, scrunching a little deeper into the sofa so his 'pillow' was smoother.

An hour later the film had finished and she still wasn't remotely sleepy. Nor had she watched much of the movie. No, she'd been completely tragic and watched him sleep— the rhythmic rise and fall of his chest, the long lashes shadowing his cheek. She was absurdly pleased he didn't snore—it wasn't as if that was relevant. It wasn't as if she was going to spend the rest of her nights sleeping beside him. Even so, she was happy. And concerned. Because he was going to get a crick in his neck if he stayed like that much longer.

She stroked his temple, loving being able to touch him so intimately. He didn't stir, so she bent forward and whispered in his ear. 'Ethan, wake up. You're going to get so uncomfortable.'

Okay, *she* was uncomfortable. It wasn't that his lying on her like this hurt, but it was hot. All she wanted was for him to wake up and play. But he was blissfully asleep and she couldn't bring herself to try harder to rouse him— especially because doubt niggled that he might not want what she wanted when he woke.

She changed the TV to a music station and lowered the volume. She rested her head on the big cushions and stroked his head, trying to match her breathing to his so she'd get to be as calm and rested as he was.

'Nadia?'

'Mmm?' Nadia sighed, lost in a really great dream.

'Nadia?'

She roused, realising that the voice was real and very amused and very near. She looked down at the heavy, warm weight in her lap.

'This is good.' He smiled. The flickering light from the TV made his eyes twinkle too. 'What are we doing here?'

'You were too heavy to move to bed.'

'You wanted me in your bed?' He shifted, rolling to face towards her tummy.

Her muscles weakened. 'Uh…um…'

'I've missed you.' His words were muffled, but still she heard the rawness. He pressed his face close to her, sliding his hands up her thighs, under the loose cotton of her boxer shorts.

Nadia shivered, half trying to suppress her tremoring nerves, but her body had lit with the lightest of touches and those few words. His hands caressed, and she couldn't help relaxing, slightly spreading her knees wider so his fingers slid higher still. She swallowed, barely able to control her breathing, high on anticipation. Oh, she wanted his touch there—all the way there.

For a moment there was nothing else—just fingertips caressing skin, slowly taking the path already on fire for him. He suddenly lifted his head and looked around the room behind them.

'What is it?' She looked up to see what was catching his attention.

'I'm looking for the treadmill,' he teased. 'You must have been exercising while I was sleeping. Your blood is pumping hot.'

In lifting his head up he'd made way for his fingers to surf even higher—which she guessed was the whole point. So Nadia just spread her legs wider.

'You've been lying with your head in my lap for the last

five hours.' Her panting mutter wasn't as saucy as she'd intended. 'I'm on fire.'

'Oh, so it's *me* making you this hot?' He lay down on her again. 'You like me this close?'

She smiled back—oh, *so* saucy now. 'I'd like it better if you were awake and I was naked.'

'Well, I am awake—but you don't need to be naked.' His touches went further, softer, teasing. One hand went north, sliding under her shirt, cupping her breasts, stroking her hard nipples. 'No bra, no knickers,' he groaned.

'Boxers are knickers,' she argued vaguely.

'Loose,' he murmured happily, his fingers pressing more firmly.

She pressed her head back on the sofa, closing her eyes and lifting her face to the ceiling. Her body was so hungry for him—all slippery and hot, welcoming the slide of his fingers, the rub of his thumb. She bit on her lip and suddenly pressed her knees close, trapping his hand as waves of pleasure contracted her muscles. It hit quick, hard, and it wasn't enough.

'Making you come is the ultimate turn-on,' he muttered as he sat up. 'And it's so damn easy.'

Uh, yeah… Struggling to regain her breath, Nadia felt embarrassment rise. It was only easy because she was so insanely attracted to him. It was humiliating.

But then she noticed he was now standing, and basically ripping off his clothes.

'What *are* you wearing?' he asked.

Her humiliation faded as she heard how he snapped the question, saw how his hands were shaking as he fought to get a handful of condoms from his pocket. So he'd been prepared to come and see her?

She knelt up on the sofa and enjoyed the show. Her body was even warmer than before. The man had muscles—everywhere—and they were all bunched. He glared at her tee shirt again. Had he only just noticed what it said?

'It's really offensive. Take it off.' His jeans thudded to the floor. 'Off, off, *off*,' he demanded.

But before she could argue he issued another order.

'Stand on the sofa.'

Nadia blinked. 'Is this because I'm short?'

A muffled curse as he moved—fast, effortlessly—lifting her so she stood in front of him on the sofa. 'No,' he said curtly, whisking her tee shirt over her head and then her boxers to her ankles. 'This is because I want to kiss you here.' He licked her nipple and then sucked it into his mouth. 'And then here.' He moved, kissing down her sternum to her stomach.

'Okay.' Oh, more than okay. Oh, yes, yes, *yes*.

Between kisses he laughed—low, sexy—making her melt all the more. His hands dropped to her thighs and he pushed them apart. She shifted her feet to please him—only he kept pushing, and pushing, until she was standing with her feet as far apart as they would go. There was something about being bossed by him that was delicious. Her body was all soft and lax and malleable, while his was all hard and strong and ready to fire, and she couldn't wait to find out how he was planning to do it.

So she stood on the sofa, her hands on his shoulders, while he stood before her, his feet on the floor. She could look him right in the eye—and his eyes were smiling. So she smiled too. His big hands held her thighs hard, keeping them wide but also giving her support. A good thing because when he suddenly thrust—all the way in—her knees buckled. She hooked her hands tighter round his neck and held on for sweet mercy. But there was no mercy—he was big, and his movements were powerful, relentless, and awesomely good.

Nadia moaned, loving the completion, the friction as their bodies slid—locking and unlocking. She thrust with him, their position incredibly decadent and abandoned, and she relished the hedonism. Every movement hit better than the last, so in seconds she was breathless and barely coping with the surging sensations. His pelvic bone ground against hers, rubbing deliciously against her bliss button, sending her faster still towards break-point. Her so-sensitive breasts were flattened against his solid chest—more fantastic friction.

But the thing short-circuiting her completely was the way they stood nose to nose and eye to eye. Unbearably intimate. He kissed her—little teasing kisses broken by the occasional lush, deep one. She could see his passion, the raw, unbridled desire. It was so intense she had to close her eyes against it. She couldn't believe that all the fiery want in his gaze was for her.

'Look at me,' he growled. 'Let me see.' As he spoke he maintained his rhythm, driving her, knowing exactly what he was doing—how close she was. How moved she was—how much she wanted him. How good he made her feel—how much more he made her want.

And that was what he wanted—she knew. He wanted to see her hit orgasm. He wanted to miss nothing. He wanted all her secret wishes—and to know that he was the one who'd fulfilled them. And just that thought—that frightening, exhilarating thought—made her come all the quicker. Because it was *him* doing this to her.

Her body tautened, then convulsed as the waves tumbled over her—so powerful that for an instant she was scared. But then it was too good to think of anything but how incredible it was. She didn't know if she cried out—all she could hear was the hiss of his satisfaction, the grit of his teeth as he held her through the rapturous storm and forced himself to stay that half-step behind her.

She sucked breaths in harder, unable to recover as he thrust more forcefully. She threaded her fingers through his hair, holding him so he couldn't look away from her either. She half laughed, mostly cried with sensual delight, as she saw the signs of unbearable strain in his face—the clenched muscles, the veins popping in his neck, the pained, desperate look in eyes that suddenly widened, but were blinded as it swamped him.

'Oh, yes,' she sobbed. Her blood pulsed—in her lips, in her most intimate nerve centre—as the sight and feel of him, so tortured by her, sent her back to the pinnacle of ecstasy.

His movements went wild. His body jerked as he lost the fight against holding off. He shouted—a raw, masculine response—as release surged and the moment of ultimate pleasure was his. All she could do then was cling.

His hands shifted, clasping round her middle, and he held on to her tightly, his forehead pressing into her shoulder. She felt his harsh, ragged breathing gusting down her sweat-soaked skin. Her own breathing was irregular, her brain dizzy. Her legs were completely wobbly. So did was her heart.

'Are you going to let me go?' she asked, her voice woefully small.

'No.' With sheer brute strength he lifted her, sliding one hand under her legs so he could carry her more comfortably. Dexterously, between his third and fourth fingers, he scooped up another condom packet that had fallen on the edge of the sofa. 'Which is your room?'

She directed him, and he walked with ridiculous ease. He placed her on the bed, but immediately followed with a smooth lunge. Taking the bulk of his weight on his elbows, he pressed his lower half firmly on hers—so she couldn't escape.

'Oh,' she said, needing to strive for some kind of control in this shattering situation. 'You want to be dominant?'

'No,' he breathed.

Nadia's voice failed as she saw his burnt brown eyes had refilled with that passionate fire. He bent his head and kissed the last remaining brain cell out of her. His tongue swept into her mouth in gliding strokes, over and over, while his hands framed her face, holding her up to him—open. Yeah right he didn't want to be dominant.

By the time he'd finished she was uncontrollably rocking her hips, grinding against him in a way that was desperate and hungry and unbelievably happy, running her hands up and down his slick, muscular back. He looked down with smug satisfaction as she panted and writhed beneath him.

His low whisper positively purred. 'You're not running out on me again.'

# CHAPTER ELEVEN

LIGHT blasted through the window and Nadia sighed, reluctantly admitting to consciousness—because now she had to face the music. She rolled over. He was awake, propped up on a pillow, book in hand—looking totally at home.

'What are you reading?' She tried to act normal, but her croaky voice let her down.

He showed her the cover. 'Found it on your shelf. It's quite good.'

Groaning, she reached down beside the bed for her phone. She had to check Megan and Sam's arrival time. She was panicking that she had their arrival time wrong and it was a.m., not p.m. The last thing she wanted was for them to walk in on her and Ethan like this. Megan would read too much into it. Nadia was having a hard enough time stopping herself from doing that.

'What are you doing?' His voice had a slightly rough inflection too—so he wasn't *that* engrossed in the book…

'Updating my profile,' she lied.

'Of course you are,' he said drily. 'What are you saying?'

She tossed the phone away, satisfied her flatmate wouldn't be arriving for another ten hours or so. 'Nothing.'

He theatrically mirrored her action, tossing the book away and faced her. The sheet slipped to reveal his broad, bronzed, way too hot, chest. 'So, Nadia, what do we do now?'

She had no idea. She'd bluff. 'Shower?'

It was a good idea. Forty minutes later there was so much steam in the bathroom the extractor fan failed. The trip switch went when it was overworked, and it was totally overworked now.

'Damn thing.' Nadia pushed her wet hair out of her face and hunted for the stool to stand on so she could fix it.

With a grin Ethan nudged her out of the way, reached up and did it for her.

She glared at him. 'Don't treat me like some incompetent little girl.'

'I'm not.' He chuckled and held her still way too easily. 'Don't project your hang-ups onto me.'

'I'm not.' She wriggled, vainly trying to escape. 'But people see me and think I'm some doll who can't manage anything on my own.'

'Honey, I'm aware of all you can manage.' His hands slipped into soft places. 'But isn't it nice to have help sometimes?'

'I don't want to be patronised. I can manage just fine alone.'

'So you won't admit to any physical limitations? But you have some, Nadia, and that's not a bad thing.'

'I refuse to be limited,' she argued. 'I can and will do anything. My parents didn't want me to move to the city— never believed I'd get a job in a big firm like Hammond. But while I may not have the size, I *do* have the smarts.'

'And you prove your power even more with your stabbing words on the internet?' He shook his head reproachfully. 'Why does it matter so much?

'You've not spent your whole life fighting the assumption that you're not as capable as the rest of the population because you're short.'

'Yeah, but proving your capability doesn't have to mean

all by yourself. You know, *some* things you have to have a partner for.' He picked her up and demonstrated just how much stronger he was—and what a 'partner' could do.

'It's not fair,' she moaned.

'Life isn't fair. Yes, I'm physically stronger than you—but there are benefits to that. Benefits you enjoy.'

She knew he was teasing, to turn her flash of anger into amusement. And it was working—because he was so right. 'Oh, really?' Her protest sounded as pathetic to her ears as it must be to his. Secretly she loved his size and strength. It was as if she'd been programmed to seek out the biggest piece of masculinity she could and cling to him. And Ethan was certainly that.

'It turns you on when I press you deep into the bed,' he muttered, kissing her neck. 'You like being lifted by me like this just as much as I like lifting you. But even big guys like me have vulnerabilities, you know. Everybody does.'

'Oh, you do?' She suspected he actually did. She just wished she knew and understood them. 'Tell me more.'

'And give you power over me?' He chuckled. 'Never.'

'You don't think I have power over you already?' She aimed to tease him back.

Their gaze met and held. And held some more.

'Why don't you find out?' he invited eventually, wickedness flaring in his eyes.

Yeah, he always brought it back to sex, didn't he? Any time the conversation got a little too close to the bone, too personal, too emotionally intimate for him, he kissed or teased his way out of it.

But right this second she was happy to let him away with it.

An hour later Ethan took another quick shower, and wandered out towel-clad to find her in front of her computer, busily tapping away. He pulled up a chair next to her and unashamedly watched her work.

'It's a pretty impressive machine.' The screen was huge.

'Yeah.' She wrinkled her nose. 'Cost a bomb.'

She was going through the million e-mails that had landed last night, checking all the comments that had been posted on WomenBWarned were okay, answering queries and direct messages. She was incredibly organised. There were tonnes of folders, the titles of which amused him—especially the 'Feedback—Excellent' and the 'Feedback—Awful' ones.

'Which one has more messages in it?' he asked, pointing to them.

'Which do you think?' She laughed, standing to answer the ringing phone. 'Oh, hi Megan…'

Ethan tuned out of her phone conversation as he read the e-mail that was next up to be sorted.

*Can you please, please, please put together a Top Ten list of the worst cheats ever on WBW? Or, even better, could we vote for them? I have THE guy to take it out on…he so deserves to be front page, number one…*

Great—another scorned and furious harpy. Shaking his head, Ethan resisted the urge to hit 'delete' and instead pulled the message into the 'suggestions' folder, as Nadia had done with the previous one on a similar theme. Then he started reading the next e-mail.

*I wanted to tell you how much I appreciate **WomanBWarned**. Not because I think all guys are scum, like the guy I dated, but because there's a place out there where someone listens and I can*

*read about other women's experiences and talk to
someone in privacy about what happened. And it
was rape. For so long I didn't know if I could call it
that—if it was my own fault or what. But it wasn't.
I didn't do anything wrong. He did. I've never told
anyone in my real life, but I have a voice on here
and you listen. It helps.*

Nadia's arm reached past him to the mouse and the
e-mail was pulled into a folder. 'Some of the messages
aren't on the public forum,' she said quietly. 'There are
some private threads.'

'Of course.' He leaned away from the screen and realised he'd been holding his breath for some unknown reason. He pushed the stale air from his lungs. 'That's awful.'

'Yeah.' Nadia sat beside him again.

'How do you know what to say to someone who's been
through that?'

She clicked through a couple more e-mails. 'It's not so
much about offering answers. I mean, what answers can
there be? There's no cute line anyone can say to fix that.
But I can give what she says—space and a place to have a
voice. I link to lots of resources, and there are other women
who've been through similar experiences who speak up.
I'm not a counsellor. I guess I facilitate. But, yeah—' she
looked glum '—some women deal with way worse than a
stupid virginity collector.'

That was true. But what had happened to Nadia had also
been horrible. And if Ethan ever came across Rafe Buxton
in real life he'd have to be forcibly restrained from doing
violence to the bastard. But if he did punch the guy out
Nadia would probably commit some form of violence on
*him*—she was so determined to take care of herself and
not have any help or protection. Especially not from a big

guy like him. As if that was the worst thing ever. But he couldn't stop that need rising in him—that *caring*.

Oh, hell. Ethan glanced at her profile and took in the shadows under her eyes. He knew she needed some recovery time and all of a sudden so did he—but it wasn't physical rest he needed, more mental and emotional. He didn't know what to think about anything any more.

'I should probably get going.' Contrarily, he instantly hoped she'd tell him to stay.

'Okay.' She nodded and kept focusing hard on the screen. 'My flatmate gets back tonight, and we've got a big catch-up planned.'

'Yeah, of course,' he said, battling disappointment and failing. He glanced briefly at the message she was reading.

*Do you think weakness can be inherited? Because I'm worried it can. For years my mum stayed with my dad, even though he cheated on her. I swore I'd never be like her—stupid enough to put up with it. But here I am and my boyfriend has cheated on me and I don't want him to leave—*

Ethan pushed away from the table, found his clothes, and went to her bedroom. He didn't want to know what Nadia's response to that one would be. Did being the son of a slimeball make you a slimeball too?

'Ethan?' Nadia stood in the doorway.

Ethan bent and pulled on his shoes, concentrating on his laces. 'My dad cheated on my mum all the time. Eventually he ran off with one of his "assistants". Then he cheated on her too. Every relationship he has, ends with him cheating. But Jess has married, and Tom is the last guy on this earth who'd do that. You should e-mail that woman and tell her. It's not some hereditary thing. Patterns don't have to repeat like that.' Not for Jess, or Polly. And not for him—because he'd made the decision to be different. Only now he didn't know if he'd been any better—if he *could* ever be any better.

Nadia blinked. 'Okay.' She took a step into the room. 'When did they divorce?'

Ethan straightened and walked back out to the lounge, picked up his bag. 'I was fourteen. It was a relief.' He wished his mother had thrown Matthew out sooner.

'Why—?'

'Nadia, I don't want to talk about it.' What did she want to know? How he'd heard his mother's tears late at night for years? How he and Jess and Polly had tried to get their father's attention and never could compete with the bright young bimbos at the studio? How Ethan had worked so hard to make his mum smile?

'I know that.' Nadia looked him square in the eye. 'But maybe you should.'

He almost smiled. But he said nothing. She really didn't want to hear his sob story. He couldn't think of a bigger turn-off. He was so much better at making her smile.

She walked with him to the door to see him off. 'Bye,' she said. 'It was...'

'Don't say *nice*.' His feelings were even more mixed-up. 'Have fun with your flatmate tonight,' he said.

'I will.' She smiled, but he could see she was biting back questions.

He didn't want to go, but she had her own friends and her own life and it was busy. So busy there wasn't as much room in it for him as he suddenly wanted. She put so much of herself into her work, her forum, her friends... So what? Now he was feeling jealous of those things? Clearly he needed more sleep.

When they'd finally sated themselves in the small hours

last night, she'd curled into a little ball and slept like the dead. He'd woken too early and waited for ages, willing her to wake up, but it had taken so long he'd had to find something to read to keep himself from bothering her. He hadn't wanted to disturb her when she looked so tired.

And he didn't want to bother her now. Much.

He bent and kissed her. The way her lips clung made him feel better. Yeah, the sex was good. And that was all he wanted, right?

Well, no. Not any more.

Dissatisfied, Ethan walked home alone. He worked for a while. Spoke to a few mates. Decided on a quiet Saturday night in—the first in ages. And he spent it in front of his computer.


Megan lounged on the sofa looking like a totally pampered cat. 'It was the best three weeks of my life,' she purred. 'The absolute best.'

Nadia laughed—three weeks sailing round the Greek Islands with a lover wouldn't be bad, would it?

'So tell me about yours?' Now Megan looked completely feline—and sly.

Nadia had tried hard to keep Megan talking about herself, but Megan wasn't being denied any longer. She had her iPad on her lap, and was scrolling through the nightmare that was Ethan's blog.

'Did you know he's put up another message?'

'He has?' Nadia's heart raced. She'd hoped they were just going to forget about the blogs. She'd been gearing up to delete hers. But there it was.

*Okay, so we're behind on the date reporting. And I'm not going to report because the reality is a whole lot more complicated than this "he said/she said" forum. I just want to pass this message on to the women out there who are reading. You want a clue into the male psyche?*

*Here it is.*

*Utterly unlike the sharing need of the female, we guys don't like to emote or analyse. Guys like action. So let us act. Let us be guys. Let us do the things we like to do for a woman.*

Well, what did *that* mean?

'Are you up for sharing, Nadia?' Megan asked, her sly tone gone quiet. And curious.

Nadia shook her head. She'd already shared way too much of herself these last twenty-four hours—with him.

# CHAPTER TWELVE

HE DIDN'T call on Sunday. Or text or e-mail or make any more comments on his blog. So she didn't either. Which wasn't to say she didn't obsess over him any time she didn't have her thoughts on a tight rein. And she worked late, late, *late* on her site.

Too early Monday morning Megan called up the stairs. 'Nadia, there's someone at the door for you.'

At seven? She went down, not trusting the wicked expression on Megan's face.

But when she got to the door she understood. Ethan, looking dynamite in casual, a combo of relaxed and confident. He all but knocked her out.

'What are you doing here?' she managed to ask.

'I thought I'd see you to your work today.'

She stared at the shiny new mountain bike beside him, still astounded to see him. 'But your work is nearer here than mine.'

'Well, I need more exercise than you.' His eyes twinkled.

'You're not serious?'

'Completely.'

Nadia's eyes narrowed. He was here, but not for the right reason. She became aware of Megan, unsubtly hunt-

ing for something in the lounge, so she could check out
Ethan some more. 'I'll just get my bag.'

Nadia backed into the house, drawing the door almost
fully closed behind her.

'Oh, Nadia.' Megan stood with arms crossed, foot tapping, and a smile wider than Australia. 'Nadia, Nadia,
Nadia.'

'No matter what you hear in the next ten minutes, do
not come outside—okay?' she instructed her friend.

Megan's eyes widened. 'Okay.'

Nadia ran to finish getting ready. She rammed her feet
into her skates and skated out through the door, banging
it behind her. She met his bright-eyed gaze as she did up
the clip on her helmet. He'd turned the bike around and
was astride, ready to push off.

Nadia moved up beside him—and then pulled her surprise.

The most horrendous, ear-splitting screeching sound
suddenly deafened them.

'What the hell is that?' Ethan shouted, looking around.

Nadia pointed to the little black rectangle tucked into
her waistband.

'It's a scream in a can,' she shouted back. 'I just pull
this cord and it makes this god-awful noise. So I don't
need a bodyguard to get to work safely, Ethan. I can take
care of myself.'

'That's not why I'm here,' he bellowed.

She silenced the screamer and stared at him, not letting
him away with it.

He sighed. 'Okay, that's a little bit of why I'm here.'

'You don't need to be here for that at all.' She waited,
brows lifted.

His mouth shut—firm—and didn't open for several
seconds. And then he blew her away.

'Look, why do you insist on pigeon-holing guys?' he demanded. 'What's with the protective/predator split—why can't I feel a bit of both? I'm quite sure you can take care of yourself, Nadia. But even if you had a black belt in karate and carried a bazooka I'd still have this random concern. It makes me feel better to be with you in the park early in the morning, okay? And what's wrong with that? Look, I'm not going to stop you from doing anything—I doubt I could. But why can't it be fun to do things together? Why do you have to prove yourself all on your own all the damn time?' He paused to swear—pithy and powerful. 'Honestly, the main reason I'm here right now is because I wanted to spend some time with you, and this is one way of sneaking in an extra half-hour. Is that a crime?'

'No.' Winded, Nadia moved forward on her skates so he couldn't see her ridiculously huge smile and her basically heaving bosom. 'That's just fine.'

But she couldn't resist glancing back—and catching his rueful, *gorgeous* smile.

It was a fantastically clear morning. She'd always loved skating. She loved how free and fast it made her feel. But skating alongside Ethan was even more of a rush. He was so right—being together made for much more fun. And he wasn't here to stop her, or because he thought she couldn't do this on her own—he actually acknowledged that she could. He was being with her right now for the pleasure of it. Adrenalin and anticipation coiled together, spinning through her veins, sending her pulse racing and her happiness meter to the sky. Because he was right. Together side-by-side like this was fantastic.

Ethan pedalled quickly, amazed at just how fast she was. And how hot. She had the leggings on, and a cute singlet top, helmet and wrist protectors. He really shouldn't be turned on by that get-up. But he was.

He'd stayed away yesterday and hated every second of the day. So now he was giving in to the nagging, all-encompassing urge to be near her. Only with her this close the urge was crippling. He wanted her more than he'd ever wanted anyone or anything, and he wanted her this instant. And he wanted more from himself—he wanted to *be* more—but he didn't know how and he hated it. Where had his carefree, walk-away attitude gone?

'I'm going to have a heart attack, exercising with you,' he muttered when they finally got to her workplace. He rested his bike against the side of the building and put his hands on his hips, trying to get his rioting body back under control. 'You have a shower in there?'

'Yes,' she said, taking off her helmet and shaking her hair loose.

'Strangers allowed?' he rasped, hormones even more wayward now.

'No.' She bit her lip and looked disappointed.

He was devastated.

But an impish look crossed her face and she leaned close to whisper in the most torturous way. 'Have you got anything with you?'

Ethan thought for a second, and his heart crashed. How could he have been so stupid as not to have a condom on him? But he'd not done this with the intention of getting some. But of course it was all he wanted right now.

Bizarrely, her expression lit up even more as she registered his dismay. 'There's a restroom in the foyer.'

So? What was the point of that when they couldn't do what he so badly wanted to do? But he followed. Couldn't *not* follow. It was so early there was no one in Reception, only a guard on the outside door, and he didn't blink when Ethan followed Nadia into the building. She went straight to a little room. Once he'd ducked in she locked the door and stepped up to him, pushing him back against it.

'You can't get back on your bike like this.' She grinned, her hands moving fast on his fly.

'Don't worry about it. I'm okay,' he said roughly. His body screamed its argument against his words. 'Really, you don't have to—'

*Oh. Oh. Oh.*

His heart stopped as she dropped before him and dived straight to party central. Everything—save that one organ—shut down. He shuddered at the hot, soft drag and pull of her mouth. Then the *not* so soft drag and pull. Her hands moved firmly—one on his shaft and the other teasing his balls. His body pounded, threatening to burst out of its skin. He ran his hands through her hair—silky and long and sweet-smelling. His head clunked hard against the door, his vision blanking out as internal sensation soared.

He should have known she'd be as passionate and whole-hearted in her efforts here as she was in every other aspect of her life. She put everything she had into everything she did—and her effort and ability totally outweighed her stature. She was a dynamo. Just being around her jolted him to life. And right now he felt more alive, more intense, more focused on one person than he ever had. Vitality streamed through his system—and unstoppable, massive force.

'Nadia,' he gritted, desperately trying to warn her. 'Nadia, *please*—'

But she ignored him, and then it was just too late. He groaned as scalding pleasure coursed through his veins, powering out of him into her hot embrace.

He hauled her up and crushed her body to his, her face into his chest, only relaxing long moments later when it occurred to him that she mightn't be able to breathe. He just wanted to hold her and absorb the zest for life that vibrated from the depths of her body. His heart thundered, slamming against the wall of his chest as if it had grown too big to be hemmed in there. Speech or anything like it was impossible. And it wasn't because of the sex. That was the really dumbfounding thing. That was the thing terrifying his tongue into knots.

Eventually she wriggled out of his arms and brushed her hair back from her face, her cheeks flushed. He stared at her, barely functioning enough to zip his pants again.

'I'd better go get changed.' She looked meaningfully at the door he was still slumped against.

'I want to see you later.' Clumsy and stupid, his words all slurred together.

'Megan will be at Sam's tonight.' The colour in her cheeks deepened.

'Great.' Then he'd be at her house.

Ten minutes later, after a cold shower, Nadia sat at her desk, phoned Megan, and told her to stay at Sam's and not come back until she'd sounded the all-clear.

By Thursday she still hadn't given her friend the signal. Ethan accompanied her home every night—and ravaged her the moment she turned the key in the lock. Once they actually got to her bedroom. Once they stumbled to the sofa again. Once he simply slammed them against the door. Later they threw together scrappy dinners, put a movie on. They'd debated and eventually agreed on action flicks—not too gory, but not dull either. They rarely got through the screenings without an intimate intermission. Between the movies, the food, and the mad, fiery sex they worked—him on his laptop, her on the computer. Until he tried to entice her to bed—to *sleep*.

'You work too much.' He stood behind her chair and wrapped his arms around her, preventing her from typing.

'You can't keep this up.' He must have felt her stiffen because he laughed and quickly corrected himself. 'Okay, I know you *can*, but it's not healthy for anyone. Most people don't do two full-time jobs at once.'

'I know,' she muttered, conceding her tiredness only because she knew he truly did believe she *could* manage. 'But I want to.'

'Is it necessary, though? Can't you ditch Hammond and just do the forum?'

'I don't really see how. And I *want* to work at Hammond. I want them to see me succeed there.'

'Nadia, you'd succeed at anything—and anyone who knows you *must* know that.'

Oh, that out-and-out statement of support so totally deserved a reward. She spun in her chair, looked up at him and smiled wickedly. 'Let's go to bed.'

But as the days passed she refused to think beyond each moment with Ethan. Surprisingly her work days flew because she threw herself into them—keeping her thoughts on that tight leash. And every second outside the office she was with him. She knew she needn't fear he was seeing anyone else as Rafe had. There simply wasn't the time. And she knew he was loyal. She'd witnessed that with his family. But she wasn't family. So she didn't talk to him about what they were doing—didn't want to hear his literally non-committal answer. His avoidance of any emotionally personal conversation. She knew she was in trouble. This was physical for him—only about the sensational sex they shared. But no matter how much they did it, the need in her didn't lessen. It worsened. And her case of "like" for him was worsening too—teetering dangerously close to that other L-word.

So her anxiety ratcheted up, and the gaping, aching hole inside her chest widened. Worse, the feeling of ecstasy didn't last as long as it had, so more and more frequently she turned back to him for the fix. She wanted more. She wanted so much *more*.

Come Friday, her nerves were fraying from sheer exhaustion—and emotional uncertainty weakened what little grip she had left. She'd had a couple of coffees and some sugar to get her through work, but seriously she was hanging out for the close of day.

But then her boss, and *his* boss, called her in for a meeting—and told her to shut the door. Nadia shot a querying look at her line manager, but he wasn't meeting her eyes. Lumps of ice infiltrated her veins, chilling her system at warp speed. Something was wrong.

'We've been going through the records for the last couple of weeks.' Her boss's boss did the talking. 'The computer records.'

Nasty-tasting spit filled her mouth. She swallowed, but it didn't go away.

'Nadia, we know you've been accessing websites that are unrelated to work. Social networks, group forums.'

'It was only a couple of times. Very quick.' Only when Ethan had rung and she'd tried to get out of the dates. Only when she'd needed to see if he'd responded… Only lots.

Her superiors were silent.

'So I'm getting a warning?' she asked, hoping for the best, her cheeks flaming hot enough to fry an egg.

'Nadia, there was content of an explicit nature on those forums.'

They'd read them. No wonder her boss wasn't looking at her. All those comments people had left on Ethan's blog. And she knew what it meant—gross misconduct. Instant dismissal.

'So you're firing me?' Her voice was thin, as if she couldn't believe it.

But inside she could. She knew that that was exactly what they were about to do. But she couldn't let it happen. She couldn't lose her reputation—everything she'd worked so hard to achieve—*the* job at *the* company in *the* biggest city. Something no one in her family had done or ever believed *she* could do.

But even as she opened her mouth to argue, they forestalled her.

'I'm sorry, Nadia. You know we have no choice.'

She did. She'd drafted the damn policy herself.

'Nadia, how could you be so careless?' Her line manager said once they'd got out into the corridor. 'You *know* there's zero tolerance—especially for...things of that nature.'

'I know.' Nadia wiped her clammy hands down the sides of her skirt. 'It's my own fault.'

But it wasn't. It was his fault. All *his* fault. Ethan and his web war and his crass friends.

She left the building only an hour later. Took a cab with her pathetic little box of personal effects. She'd lasted less than six months. If she didn't get another job she wouldn't be able to pay her rent. Megan was going to move out soon anyway—Nadia just knew it. Megan and Sam were so together and so serious and so happy.

And what was Nadia doing? Screwing around with a jerk who didn't give a damn about anything other than having a bit of fun. She and he weren't *together*, they weren't serious, and Nadia most certainly wasn't happy. Her career was finished, and so was her fling.

She sent him a text.

*Don't bother meeting me at work. I've left early.*

Her phone rang three seconds later.

'Are you okay? Why have you left early?' he asked the second she answered.

'It wasn't my choice,' she snarled into the phone.

'What?'

'I've just been sacked.'

*'What?'*

'Gross misconduct. For accessing inappropriate material on the internet. Your blog.'

There was a silence. Then, 'Where are you?'

'Home. I don't want to see you.'

But he'd already hung up.

Twenty minutes later he was pounding on her door and calling for her to let him in. She unlocked the door and glared at him. He pushed past her. She saw him glance at her box of belongings from Hammond.

'Nadia…' His tone was too warm—trying too hard to soothe.

And the thing was she *did* want soothing. Her anger dropped the second she saw him and she wanted a hug. She wanted him to tell her it didn't matter, that it was all going to be okay. She wanted him to tell her he cared.

But she was terrified he wasn't going to. 'I don't want to see you right now.' She was hot, shaking, mortified that she wanted his support so badly and sure she wasn't going to get it.

'You're blaming me?' The soothing bit dropped from his voice.

'Who else?'

'Oh, I don't know.' He faced her, and to her utter incredulity he was *smiling*. 'How about yourself?'

Her stupid eyes flooded with acid tears that burned and made them water all the more. She turned her back on him quickly to hide them.

'Nadia—'

His hands settled on her shoulders and she quickly moved forward out of reach. 'I *hate* you.'

'You don't hate *me*.' She could still hear his smile. 'You hate how much you want me.'

She gasped. So, what? It was only *her* wanting *him* that much? That was exactly what she'd been afraid of. 'You're the most arrogant prick I've ever met.' Even if he was right.

'Nadia.' He walked towards her, his eyes hot enough to melt Antarctica.

She stood her ground and snarled, 'You think you'll make it all better with sex? You think that'll make everything okay? Have a quick screw and then be gone? That's your whole attitude, isn't it?' It was on that level that he saw everything and tried to fix everything.

And, yes, she wanted him, but she didn't want just that from him. All the uncertainty and stress of the week compounded, multiplied, and made everything in her vision wobble like just-set jelly.

'No.' He stopped and sighed. 'I just don't think this is the calamity you think it is.'

'Not the calamity—?' Her jaw dropped. 'It's a catastrophe. You've messed up my life completely. I hope you're satisfied.'

'Nadia, be honest,' he said drily. 'You weren't into that job anyway. You were only there to prove to everyone you could get a job at a firm like that—because you were dumb enough to think people didn't think you were capable of it.' The sensual invitation in his demeanour dropped, and suddenly he looked all serious. 'The fact is your heart has never been in it. You resent the time you have to be there. You give it your best—because you're incapable of giving anything less—but there are a million things you'd rather be doing. It's just that you're too chicken to do them. You're scared of failing. That's why you wouldn't ever identity yourself on WomanBWarned. You're a coward.'

She couldn't believe he didn't get how devastating this

was. She couldn't believe he didn't acknowledge his own responsibility for this mess and its seriousness. She wanted him to feel the hurt she was feeling. She wanted him to be sorry and show her he cared for her in a way other than sexual. But he didn't. Hell, she *did* need protection—from herself, for being as naïve as the kid people sometimes mistook her for. For hoping there was more to their relationship.

'*You're* calling *me* a coward?' she yelled at him. 'You—the guy who *never* takes any risks? You only ever sail in easy waters—avoiding real conflict by keeping any relationship on a sexual footing and never going any deeper.' She snatched a breath and charged full scorn ahead. 'You don't date anyone long enough to get to know them. You don't invest anything. Certainly you don't build trust and *talk* to anyone. Then you skip on to find someone else, ensuring you've left things easy with the last lover. My website hit-rate matters to me, but it's nothing on what *you* need from your followers in real life. You send flick-off flowers so those women are left half in love with you and wondering what the hell is wrong with them.'

'Nothing's wrong with them,' he shouted back at her. 'But I told you I don't want complications or scenes.'

'Or commitment.' She said the one word he never had. 'So you escape before it can arise. You hide behind superficial charm. You don't *want* to care. You're as bad as your dad.'

'I'm not,' he roared. 'I don't cheat—'

'But you *hurt* people,' she interrupted furiously. 'You *have*.' He was now.

'You think I don't know that?' His voice rose even more. 'You think I haven't realised a few new things in this last week? Give me some credit, Nadia.'

'Why? When you can't even admit that I'm in a mess

and that you're partly responsible? When all you can offer is a quick frolic like that's a Band-Aid to fix everything? Yes, I stuffed up—but so did you. And you still are.'

He lifted his hands, shaking them in frustration. 'What do you want from me? I'm here, aren't I? I've been here all week. Doesn't that count for something?'

'What have you been here for, Ethan?' Panting, she fought back the weak tears as she challenged him. 'What have you been here *for*?'

'Well, what have *you* been taking?' he sneered. 'You can't get enough of what I've been offering.'

She shook her head. 'I was stupid enough to try it your way. To throw caution to the wind—'

'You're crippled by caution,' he shouted over the top of her. 'It's so easy for you to believe the worst of me, isn't it? Because you're so untrusting. But the person you trust least is yourself.'

'Yeah? Well, what about you? Who do *you* trust? You say guys don't like to share—but that's the most pathetic excuse, and what little you offer isn't enough. So your father's a bastard? Why not open up and get over it? You're the one who needs to vent the bad stuff out.'

'Oh, like you have? Like you've *so* moved on from having some guy screw you over? Yeah, Nadia—you're so whole and healthy you've decided you won't ever need anyone or anything. You can't even let yourself rely on someone else to reach up and flick a switch for you.'

At that Nadia hurled the worst she could at him. 'At least I *care* about the things and the people in my life. I don't want to be like you. I don't want to skim through, not feeling anything other than a cheap thrill every now and then.' She'd lost everything over something that to him was *nothing*.

He stood very still, staring at her with eyes that had

darkened from brown to black. 'So all we've been is a cheap thrill?'

'At best,' she snapped, hurt into hyperbole and the denial of her own deeply precious feelings. 'And all I want now is for you to get out of my life and stay out of it.'

# CHAPTER THIRTEEN

*The point of this blog was for guys to get wise. Of
course the guy who really needed to wise up was
this one. Ladies, you can celebrate—Mr 3 Dates and
You're Out has got what was coming to him.*
   *She's ended it with me. And it's hell.*

ETHAN stared at the black characters on the screen so long
his eyes hurt. Okay, the rest of him hurt too. His life had
never sucked so much as it did right now—and right now
he couldn't see a way to make it better. He'd been in uncharted waters with Nadia—from the moment he'd met her
she'd been everything unexpected. It had been as awful
and infuriating as it had wonderful. And it had only grown
all the more wonderful. And awful.

She hadn't got the message he'd left on the blog the
other day—about letting his actions speak. Instead she'd
misread his actions, and he guessed he couldn't blame her
for that when he'd been too afraid to verbalise them even
to himself. He'd never felt this way about anyone before,
and he was feeling his way blind. But he'd been trying,
damn it—wanting to do more and be more and go further
with her than he ever had with another woman. He'd he
spent every moment he could with her—wasn't that car-

ing? What more did she want? This wasn't a hook-up for him. It was so much more than sex.

But not, apparently, for her. For her this *was* merely a cheap thrill. Yet she'd said she wanted to care—she *did* care about things—so passionately his own blood burned in response to equal hers. So why couldn't she care about *him*? Was he that unlikeable? That unlovable?

Well, yeah, at heart that was what he was most afraid of. That she'd gotten to know more about him in the last few days and he wasn't enough—like she'd said in her blog. There was nothing but superficial charm that faded.

Since his teens he'd worked so hard to ensure no one else would ever leave him—being a charming, entertaining brother and son. Being a super-nice date for women— women he'd left before they left him. He'd worried that if he wasn't the charming nice guy no one would want to know what was underneath.

With Nadia nothing had followed the usual pattern. They'd been playing a stupid game, flaming their antagonism and attraction, and it had come to matter more than everything else in his life. But old habits died hard, and when he'd been confronted with her looking that pale, her green eyes watering, his instinct had been to hold her and make her smile however he could. And he knew how much Nadia enjoyed his touch. So maybe he'd come on too teasing? Maybe he should have offered a no-thrills hug? But when she'd rejected him so furiously he'd been cut to the quick and retaliated right back. Too hard. Telling her the things he thought with zero subtlety or cushioning. And she'd responded in kind—couldn't have made it clearer.

For the first time Ethan had been dumped by a woman. And it hurt way worse than he'd ever thought it could because he'd offered so much more to her than to anyone.

He'd been trying to give her himself—in his own time. But it seemed that was so little she hadn't even realised.

He looked at the words he'd typed into the computer— they mocked him with their uselessness. There was no point in writing anything. She wasn't ever going to believe him—*in* him.

Once, twice, a hundred times, he slowly depressed the "delete" button.

Nadia curled in her chair, hugging her knees to her chest, staring at the screen and the blogs Ethan had posted to tease the hell out of her only a week ago. There was nothing new and there was no point looking. No wonder the good feeling had been fading faster—there had been no emotional foundation. At least not from him. Her doubts had only grown as the days had passed, and she'd been right to feel them. Now she knew she wasn't one to have flings. She couldn't "use" anyone like that. She only ended up used herself. Just as she'd been with Rafe. She *couldn't* trust her own judgement.

She heard the ping of e-mails landing and toggled the screen. A few messages on WomanBWarned that she skimmed—then she shot her feet to the floor and leaned close to the screen. Sandwiched between the usual comments were two e-mails that sent adrenalin shrieking down her veins.

*CaffeineQueen* and a couple of messages later *MinnieM*— two of the women who'd posted on the original thread. They'd finally replied to the e-mail she'd sent the night she'd thought Ethan had stood her up. She hesitated, heart battering her ribs. She held her breath and clicked the first.

Total disappointment. There was only a repetition of the same spiel that she'd first put up on the thread—no more detail, no more comment. Nadia frowned and opened the other one.

Same deal. Still, what had she expected? To feel some kind of kinship with these women? She stared for a moment, absently looking at the details at the top—the time it was sent, the date, the name and address...

Wait a minute...

Nadia flicked back to the first e-mail from *CaffeineQueen*. A cold, wet feeling slithered down her spine. She checked *MinnieM*. Then checked again in case she'd made a mistake. But no.

While both e-mails had different names, the actual e-mail address in the pointed brackets was the same.

Two online identities and domains traced back to one e-mail address. One woman.

Nadia's skin prickled. Tears sprang as the ramifications clanged round her bruised body. So simple. So awful. She'd been so stupid.

She thought back to that very first, fraught meeting she'd had with Ethan, when he'd suggested that her site was open to abuse, to someone taking advantage of it. He'd been right. And she'd been wrong. So very, very wrong.

And all she'd done since was yell at him. Blame him. Hurt him. And why? Because she'd been upset that he didn't care about her the way she'd come to care for him so quickly?

Well, that was her problem. Not his. And he didn't deserve to have borne her fury. Most likely he didn't deserve this other woman's fury either. Oh, hell. She had to tell him. She had to make it up to him.

And she had to do it now.

With three clicks of his mouse Ethan deleted his entire blog. He hated that she'd lost her job. He'd never intended that she be hurt like this. Yes, he'd wanted to teach her a lesson—but not total her life. And instead of him teaching her anything, she'd made him question everything about *his* life—and he didn't like the answers he was coming up with. All he wanted now was to get her back. She was already lodged in his heart and there was no getting her out of there. He'd never had to get a woman back before—until now he'd never wanted to.

Somehow he figured flowers weren't going to cut it. He was just going to have to become the kind of man she wanted. A man with depth. A man not afraid to take risks—the risk of commitment. A man not afraid to open up and talk.

Well, he'd take a risk now—put his neck on the block for her to take a swing at again.

He banged on her door. It wasn't that late. Knowing her, she'd be awake.

A woman answered, but not the one he wanted. 'You're Megan.' The flatmate.

She didn't look surprised to see him. But she didn't smile. 'She's not here.'

His stomach dropped. 'Where is she?'

'Gone to see you.'

'Oh.' He stiffened to stop from sagging. He'd gone that boneless. 'My place?'

He hardly noticed her nod. He was running back down the path to catch the cab that had already gone part-way down the street, telling the driver to floor it once he was inside.

Nadia was hovering on the footpath outside his place. He didn't know if she'd knocked already or not, but she looked about to run, so he grabbed her hand and made use of his superior strength. Only the physical pressure wasn't necessary—she walked beside him, even walked in ahead of him, slipping her hand free as she did so.

It wasn't until they were both inside and he was standing between her and the door that he said anything. His internal organs were working overtime to process the anxiety swamping his system—because she didn't look good. 'Are you okay?'

'I'm sorry to bother you,' she answered, like an automaton. 'Do you have a minute?'

'What's happened?'

He really needed to know. *Now.* Because she clearly wasn't here to get back with him. She looked as if her world had fallen apart—all pale and shivery and scared.

She bit her lip. 'I did some research. I should have done it sooner.' A tear trickled over.

'What research?' He forced himself to stand back—not to swamp her in his arms as he ached to. This time he had to *listen* and then *talk.*

'I e-mailed the women who'd posted on your thread.'

He froze, dropping his eyes from her to the floor as he absorbed that. *So* not what he'd expected.

'It was when I thought you'd stood me up and I was mad with you,' she said quickly.

'And they wrote back?' He measured his breathing—and his reply.

'*She* did.' Nadia's voice cracked. 'It was only one woman. She'd made up another log-in. I checked and found she'd done all the others too. I think she made it up.'

Ethan still couldn't look at her, because seeing Nadia this cut up tore him apart. If he snuck even another glance he'd be over there and stuffing things up again.

'So you were right.' She spoke so softly he hardly heard her words—but he heard the heartbreak.

He shoved his hands in his pockets, feeling more sorry for her than he did for himself.

'How many others are on there, making up rubbish?' she asked, not seeming to expect an answer because she went straight on, her distress becoming more audible. 'I really believed in it. I really did.'

'I know.'

'I'm so sorry, Ethan. I've already shut down the thread. I'm going to shut down the whole site—I just need to give the members some warning.'

She was broken.

Only a couple of weeks ago he'd have been punching the air and yahooing about the site being pulled. Laughing. He'd never felt less like laughing.

'I don't want you to shut it down.' She really was an idealist, wasn't she? Believing in the best of people—except for "men like him", of course. Believing she could make a difference. And she could—she really, really could. But being such an idealist meant she could also be crushed— as she was now. 'Don't shut it down.'

'I have to. This makes it worthless.'

'No, it doesn't. You can't kill all that effort. I saw some of those e-mails. And there were so many other e-mails in those folders. You help people. Just because one woman abused your system it doesn't mean you should ditch all the others by shutting down the site. Just like the fact that one guy took advantage of you in the past shouldn't put you off all the rest.' He *really* didn't want her to be put off.

'But it was you she hurt. It was *you*.'

'And that makes it worse?' His whisper was as soft as hers.

'Yes.'

His heart beat unbearably fast, and his eyes stung as if wind had blown sand in them. But he jammed his hands deeper into his pockets, determined to be *honest* and open up to her. 'Nadia, what's on that thread about me is right.'

'No, it's not.'

'It *is* true,' he argued, aching inside. 'I guess that's really why it bothered me so much when I first saw it.' He looked up at her. 'Whether I actually went out with that woman I don't know. But what she said was right—I was shallow. I was arrogant. I played—' He broke off and laughed painfully. 'And what you said earlier was even more true. I thought I had it together. My life was settled and easy. And empty. I love my job, but I shied away from relationships because they were too much work. I didn't want to be like Dad and neglect a woman by spending all my time at work, or cheat. I told myself I was okay because I dated only one at a time. Always nice, never arguing. But really I was just like him. Knowing how to take advantage. Not having the fibre or the soul to commit. I *used* those women. I was shallow to think that everyone was having a good time and no one was being hurt.'

He couldn't look her in the eyes now, couldn't face the condemnation he deserved. 'But you want to know the real pathetic truth, Nadia? You want to know why I didn't go for more than three dates? Because I didn't want to be hurt. You know, he walked out and I still wonder why. Why didn't he want us? Why hasn't anything I've done been enough to get his affection or attention? I know it shouldn't matter. I know it's his loss—but I still feel it. And I hate that rejection. I hate that it matters so much. I don't want to feel it again. I don't want to let anyone have that power over me,' he mumbled. 'But then I met you, and I've had it so wrong. You make me want so many things I never thought I'd want.'

Nadia moved three paces towards him, desperately wanting to touch him but too scared because he still stood so defensively—all shut away and retreating from her. 'Ethan—'

'Please don't come near me. If I touch you now I won't tell you all the things I need to tell you. I'm sorry, okay? I'm sorry.'

But he didn't need to be. 'Ethan, you're nothing like your father.' She tried to swallow the burning lump in her throat so she could speak clearly. 'You're a fantastic son and brother and uncle. You're loyal, you're dependable— there for them when they need you. You know just how to make them smile and feel better. You bring sunshine to their world and that's such a skill. That's not superficial. I'm sorry I said you were. Because you're not. You care too, Ethan.'

He still stared hard at the floor. 'But I've never cared about anyone the way I care about you.' His voice dropped to almost inaudible. 'I've never wanted a woman the way I want you.'

Her breathing ratcheted. The goosebumps of old feathered across her skin. She couldn't move.

'You're the most passionate person I've ever met. And I'm don't mean sex.' Beneath his tee shirt his biceps flexed. Then he lifted his head and drilled those fiery eyes right though her. 'Whatever it is you take on, you pour everything you can into it. Yes, you make the odd mistake—but so what? You also achieve amazing things. I love the energy you have for *everything* you do in life. I want to be like that.' His hands jerked out of his pockets as he suddenly strode towards her. 'But sometimes it seems like you don't need anyone or anything. You're so determined to get out there and achieve it all on your own.'

Was that what he thought? Her heart wrung—he was so wrong.

'But you *do* need people.' He bent, grasping her upper

arms. 'And you *want* to be valued. You want to be loved, and you should be—just for you.'

She didn't bother trying to hide the tears slipping down her cheeks. She just wiped them with uselessly wet fingers.

'You *are* valued, Nadia. You *are* loved.' His voice dropped to a whisper. '*I* love you.'

'You don't.' He couldn't. He just couldn't.

He looked distressed and his fingers tightened. 'Please believe in me. In us. In yourself. I know there's courage in you, Nadia. Please trust me.'

'But I've been such a bitch. You can't possibly like me when I've been so horrible.'

The desperate pinch in his features lessened. So did the pressure on her arms. 'Well, I've been a jerk too.' A smile flashed then. 'And, yeah, there've been a couple of seconds when I didn't *like* you—but I absolutely love you and I always will.'

It was a mountain blocking her throat now, so she couldn't speak at all. She couldn't actually think. There was just amazement and disbelief and relief and the sweetest warm feeling trickling through her.

'WomanBWarned does a lot of good things. Put in a few more checks and balances, Nadia. Make it better. Don't destroy it. And let me *help* you—not because I don't think you can do it on your own, but because I *care*. Let me be beside you, cheering all the way.'

She smiled, the block in her throat melting. 'You don't want to be involved in WomanBWarned.'

'Yes, I do—because it matters to you and I can see what it could be.' He sighed. 'It doesn't matter what any of those people think about me...' He hesitated, looking almost shy as he muttered, 'All that matters is what *you* think of me.'

A rainbow burst in her chest, flooding her with colour and warmth and light—and, yes, *courage*. Real genuine courage to go for what she truly wanted. 'Ethan, I think the world of you.' She stretched up on tiptoe as if she could make him believe her if she was closer. 'You're the sunshine, the air—you're everything to me. I love you.'

He smiled, but in his eyes there was still a scared look. 'Really?'

'It shouldn't be so hard to believe.' She ran her fingers down the hard planes of his chest. 'Let me prove it to you.'

He covered her hand with his and stopped its journey down his flinching abs. 'I don't want to think we're just about sex. I mean, it's the best *ever* with you, but there's more to us than—'

'I know that.' She put her fingers over his mouth. 'Take me to bed, please, Ethan—and *make love* with me.'

Still he hesitated. 'I thought you didn't want to…'

His bedroom. She remembered now—she'd been such a bitch she'd refused to go into his room last time she was here. 'Those women are a part of your past,' Nadia said. 'I might not like it that much, but I do accept it. Just like you're willing to accept WomanBWarned.'

'You know I'm only interested in one woman now,' he said seriously. 'And there weren't really that many notches.' His eyes suddenly danced. 'And last week I got a new bed anyway. I thought I'd turn over a new bedspread.'

'Instead of a new leaf?'

'Yeah.' He held her closer still. 'And it's so much better than I'd ever have believed.'

'So I'm going to be the first in your new bed?' she teased.

'And the last.'

He hoisted her up and she wound her legs round his waist. He moved quickly. They stripped quickly. But when they lay down they both intuitively slowed. It was lovemaking at its simplest—face-to-face, arms entwined. The moment of completion was sublime. She clamped her legs together, locking him inside her. He kissed her deeply so they were as close and connected as possible, taking up only the narrowest space in the super-size bed.

'I love you,' he whispered again.

She answered him over and over, until ecstasy hit and sent her to paradise. Clinging to him tightly, she took him with her. She rested on him after, coasting her hand down his chest, joyously free to caress him as she pleased. And she was *so* pleased—so in love.

'Let's go on a date.' She lifted her head, energised by a resurgence of elation. 'We could go dancing—I'd love to dance with you.'

'No. I'm not ever going on a date with you again. Not ever.'

She stared down at him, her breath catching.

'Neither of us are in the dating scene, okay?' he said intently. 'We're in a *relationship*.'

'A what?'

'You heard.' He grinned—although it was a little short on his usual confidence and heavier on self-consciousness. 'You're the woman I want to be with. The only woman. Whatever it takes, Nadia. Even—' he breathed deep '—commitment.'

She clapped a hand over her mouth to hide her giggle of incredulity—and of delight—because there was no doubting his sincerity.

He grabbed her wrist and pulled it back so he could see her smile and kiss it. 'You and I both knew the minute we laid eyes on each other that we were going to end up in bed together,' he said huskily. 'Now we're just staying there the rest of our lives.'

'In bed?'

He rolled his eyes. 'And you accuse *me* of wanting only

one thing?' But he nudged his hips up, pressing between her thighs and proving that he, too, still wanted *that* as much as ever.

Nadia reached her arms round him and hugged him as close as she could, amazed to discover that she could feel so happy. It surged and swamped and then radiated out of her. It couldn't be contained. He gave her the confidence, the certainty she craved—not just with his actions, but now with words too. His actions had been telling her for days what she'd been too chicken to believe. He'd been there for her. He'd wanted her, challenged her as much as helped her, made her laugh as much as he'd made her mad, and she loved him more passionately than she'd ever thought possible. With him, her heart was infinitely huge.

And finally she could truly believe—he was strong, supportive, sexy and *hers*.

'I won't let you down, Nadia,' he whispered, his expression filled with pure liquid promise.

'I know.' She framed his face between her palms. 'I won't let you down either. It's going to be fun.'

He smiled, his face as handsomely charming as ever, and full of inner emotion. 'It's going to be for ever.'

### *WomanBWise!*

*I'm Nadia Keenan—formerly **OlderNWiser** on **WomanBWarned**. I know we've been counting down to our whole new look for a few weeks now, and I'm so thrilled to be able to unveil it today!*

*First up—you've noticed the change in name, right?*

*I know my old ID said I was wiser—fact was, I wasn't. I'm still not. There's so much I have to*

*learn... We all do, right? But we can get there to-
gether...*

*So, welcome to the launch of **WomanBWise**.
I hope you like the new format, I think it's pretty
easy to navigate your way round. We've incorpo-
rated several of your suggestions from our "feedback frenzy", and we've added in a few new ideas
of our own. There are a couple more boxes to fill in
when you register, but we think it's worth the extra
five seconds. And remember your privacy is important to us. We don't share your personal info with
any third parties.*

*Some exciting new features include our online
shop—you can get our too-cute tee shirts, and we
also have a very nifty personal alarm that's little
enough to conceal in the tiniest of evening bags—
or, even better, on yourself. And if you're a girl who
likes bubbles at a party, be sure to pick up one of
our cute bottle stops that fits onto your mini-bottle.
You sip through a straw so there's no chance of your
drink being spiked. It fits soda and juice bottles too
and, again, will tuck into your purse super-easy.*

*Our personal safety items aren't about being
paranoid, but about being prepared when you get
your party shoes on. We're all about making smart,
strong, safe choices. And we're about building a sis-
terhood that supports. Mr 3 Dates and You're Out
was right—we women do love to share. And so we
should—the good as well as the bad!*

*Yes, there's a new section for your best date des-
tination ideas, and a section for success stories—
there's one up there already. You might have read
about them before...they had a little blog war going
for a while there ;)*

*Dating, dancing, going to dinner and meeting new people should be a fun and positive experience. But sometimes it doesn't work out. Sometimes bad stuff happens. So let's listen, clue each other in, and learn—so we can move forward and maybe make fewer mistakes...*

*And as you all begged for it, there will be a regular blog from Mr 3 Dates—our man from the dark side. I know how popular his views are with you all!*

*Meanwhile, he and I are now up to date number 128. Yes, I know its only three months since our first dreadful movie date, but we've been having a few two-date days. Actually, Ethan insists we're no longer dating, but that we're in a relationship. He's given me a diamond to try to prove it.*

*But we are dating—because how can I run a dating divas support centre if I'm not dating?*

*Oh okay—to settle his nerves, I confess online, in public and unreservedly, that I'll be dating him the rest of my life...*

*Which just goes to show that even the burnt-by-boys girl and the scared-to-settle guy can get over it when they meet the right one for them...*

*So get out there, get dating, and have some safe, sexy fun. If fate has her way you'll find your one when you least expect it. But, no matter what, remember that we're all here to help, listen and laugh along the way—and we'll be wise women together! Love, Nadia.*

**COMING NEXT MONTH from Harlequin Presents® EXTRA**
AVAILABLE OCTOBER 30, 2012

### #221 A NIGHT IN THE PALACE
*A Christmas Surrender*
**Carole Mortimer**
When Giselle Barton flies to Rome at Christmas, the last thing she expects is to be kidnapped by the demanding and sinfully attractive Count Scarletti!

### #222 JUST ONE LAST NIGHT
*A Christmas Surrender*
**Helen Brooks**
One last night of heady passion with her husband is too much for Melanie Masterson to resist...but it comes with an unexpected consequence....

### #223 CRACKING THE DATING CODE
*Battle of the Sexes*
**Kelly Hunter**
Poppy thought she would be safe on a desert island, until she meets the owner—and he's the most dangerously sexy man she's ever seen.

### #224 HOW TO WIN THE DATING WAR
*Battle of the Sexes*
**Aimee Carson**
Helping to arrange a celebrity dating event should be easy for Jessica, but Cutter Thompson's sexy smile has her breaking every rule in her relationship book!

# REQUEST YOUR
# FREE BOOKS!

**Harlequin** *Presents*

## 2 FREE NOVELS PLUS
# 2 FREE GIFTS!

PASSION GUARANTEED SEDUCTION

---

**YES!** Please send me 2 FREE Harlequin Presents® novels and my 2 FREE gifts (gifts are worth about $10). After receiving them, if I don't wish to receive any more books, I can return the shipping statement marked "cancel." If I don't cancel, I will receive 6 brand-new novels every month and be billed just $4.30 per book in the U.S. or $4.99 per book in Canada. That's a saving of at least 14% off the cover price! It's quite a bargain! Shipping and handling is just 50¢ per book in the U.S. and 75¢ per book in Canada.* I understand that accepting the 2 free books and gifts places me under no obligation to buy anything. I can always return a shipment and cancel at any time. Even if I never buy another book, the two free books and gifts are mine to keep forever.

106/306 HDN FERQ

| | |
|---|---|
| Name | (PLEASE PRINT) |

| | |
|---|---|
| Address | Apt. # |

| | | |
|---|---|---|
| City | State/Prov. | Zip/Postal Code |

Signature (if under 18, a parent or guardian must sign)

### Mail to the **Reader Service:**
**IN U.S.A.:** P.O. Box 1867, Buffalo, NY 14240-1867
**IN CANADA:** P.O. Box 609, Fort Erie, Ontario L2A 5X3

Not valid for current subscribers to Harlequin Presents books.

**Are you a current subscriber to Harlequin Presents books
and want to receive the larger-print edition?
Call 1-800-873-8635 or visit www.ReaderService.com.**

\* Terms and prices subject to change without notice. Prices do not include applicable taxes. Sales tax applicable in N.Y. Canadian residents will be charged applicable taxes. Offer not valid in Quebec. This offer is limited to one order per household. All orders subject to credit approval. Credit or debit balances in a customer's account(s) may be offset by any other outstanding balance owed by or to the customer. Please allow 4 to 6 weeks for delivery. Offer available while quantities last.

---

**Your Privacy**—The Reader Service is committed to protecting your privacy. Our Privacy Policy is available online at www.ReaderService.com or upon request from the Reader Service.

We make a portion of our mailing list available to reputable third parties that offer products we believe may interest you. If you prefer that we not exchange your name with third parties, or if you wish to clarify or modify your communication preferences, please visit us at www.ReaderService.com/consumerschoice or write to us at Reader Service Preference Service, P.O. Box 9062, Buffalo, NY 14269. Include your complete name and address.

---

*Discover the magic of the holiday season in*
*SLEIGH RIDE WITH THE RANCHER,*
*an enchanting new Harlequin® Romance story*
*from award-winning author Donna Alward.*

*Enjoy a sneak peek now!*

\* \* \*

"BUNDLE UP," he suggested, standing in the doorway. "Night's not over yet."

A strange sort of twirling started through her tummy as his gaze seemed to bore straight through to the heart of her. "It's not?"

"Not by a long shot. I have something to show you. I hope. Meet me outside in five minutes?"

She nodded. It was their last night. She couldn't imagine *not* going along with whatever he had planned.

When Hope stepped outside she first heard the bells. Once down the steps and past the snowbank she saw that Blake had hitched the horses to the sleigh again. It was dark but the sliver of moon cast an ethereal glow on the snow and the stars twinkled in the inky sky. A moonlight sleigh ride. She'd guessed there was something of the romantic in him, but this went beyond her imagining.

The practical side of her cautioned her to be careful. But the other side, the side that craved warmth and romance and intimacy…the side that she'd packaged carefully away years ago so as to protect it, urged her to get inside the sleigh and take advantage of every last bit of holiday romance she could. It was fleeting, after all. And too good to miss.

HREXP1112R

Blake sat on the bench of the driver's seat, reins in his left hand while he held out his right. "Come with me?"

She gripped his hand and stepped up and onto the seat. He'd placed a blanket on the wood this time, a cushion against the hard surface. A basket sat in between their feet and Blake smiled. "Ready?"

Ready for what? She knew he meant the ride but right now the word seemed to ask so much more. She nodded, half exhilarated, half terrified, as he drove them out of the barnyard and on a different route now—back to the pasture where they'd first taken the snowmobile. The bells called out in rhythm with hoofbeats, the sound keeping them company in the quiet night.

\* \* \*

*Pick up a copy of SLEIGH RIDE WITH THE RANCHER by Donna Alward in November 2012.*

*And enjoy other stories in the Harlequin® Romance* HOLIDAY MIRACLES *trilogy:*

*SNOWBOUND IN THE EARL'S CASTLE by Fiona Harper • Available now*

*MISTLETOE KISSES WITH THE BILLIONAIRE by Shirley Jump • December 2012*

Find yourself
**BANISHED TO THE HAREM**
in a glamorous and tantalizing new tale from

# *Carol Marinelli*

Playboy Sheikh Prince Rakhal Alzirz has time for
one more fling in London before he must return
to his desert kingdom—and Natasha Winters has
caught his eye. He seizes the chance to discover if
Natasha is as fiery in bed as her flaming red hair,
but their recklessness has consequences.... She
might be carrying the Alzirz heir!

# BANISHED TO THE HAREM

**Available October 16!**

www.Harlequin.com

HPI3I03